9: LUCE'S BIG MISTAKE

I ate my apple as slowly as I could because the hunger pangs were so awful I could hardly bear them. I began to weaken. I was on duty at the café after school. I daydreamed about having a huge burger and chips, but then I looked at Jaimini, who had lain back on the grass because the sun was nice and hot. She looked like a model or something. The same jealous pang pierced me and brought back my resolution to be thin – in fact, the thinnest of us all.

Also in the Café Club series by Ann Bryant

The CAFÉ Club

9: LUCE'S BIG MISTAKE

Ann Bryant

Hippo

With grateful thanks to
Vanessa Morley and Rob Darracott

Scholastic Children's Books,
Commonwealth House, 1–19 New Oxford Street,
London WC1A 1NU, UK
a division of Scholastic Ltd
London ~ New York ~ Toronto ~ Sydney ~ Auckland

First published by Scholastic Ltd, 1997

Copyright © Ann Bryant, 1997

ISBN 0 590 19343 0

Typeset by TW Typesetting, Midsomer Norton, Avon

Printed by Cox & Wyman Ltd, Reading, Berks.

All rights reserved

10 9 8 7 6 5 4 3 2 1

The right of Ann Bryant to be identified as the author
of this work has been asserted by her in accordance with the
Copyright, Designs and Patents Act, 1988.

Chapter 1

Hi. I'm Luce. Unfortunately.

When you're stuck with a name like Luce, believe me you come in for one big crateful of abuse. Hey! That rhymes, doesn't it? Maybe I'm following in Mum's footsteps. She's always writing poetry. She's obsessed with it. Oops, I've gone off the point already. I'm sorry, I can't help it. It's because I'm the crazy one, I suppose. I can't say I'm any more over the moon with my image than I am with my name, but unfortunately I'm stuck with them both. I'll tell you why.

I've got these five really good friends, and the label "the crazy one" comes from them. We've all got labels. For example, my best friend is Jaimini (which you pronounce Jay-m-nee) Riva and she's known as the brainy one. She's also really good-looking, the lucky thing, with long black straight hair and lovely dark skin because of having a black father and a white mother. So while I'm

1

fickle with freckles, Jaimini's beautiful with brains. Does that sound fair to you?

It doesn't matter which friend I describe next, they *all* come out sounding better than me. Oh, well. (Huge sigh.) I'll start with Fen because she's the sort of kingpin. Her aunt Jan is the manageress of *The Café* in Cableden, where we all live and go to school. Fen got us all jobs in Jan's café. So, one of us works on Monday after school for two hours, the next Tuesday, and so on. The sixth person gets to do four hours on a Saturday, so we rotate the days we work each week to make things fair.

The thing is, as we're all thirteen, there's no way our mums would let us work more hours than that, so the Café Club, as we call it, was the most brilliant brainwave of Fen's. Her real name's Fenella Brooks and she's the ambitious one. She's medium height and resembles a stick insect. (That's one of my ambitions, by the way, to be like a stick insect.) She's got light brown, shoulder-length hair and freckles. Thank goodness *one* of my friends has got freckles.

Fen's best friend is Natasha Johnston, or Tash for short, and she's the peacemaker. It's impossible not to like Tash. She's so sweet and kind and thoughtful. Her hair is very dark and she's got lovely laughing eyes and very thick eyebrows. I only mention that because I've got very thick eyebrows too, and it makes me feel

2

better if I think other people have got to put up with the odd bad feature. It's just a shame that I seem to be entirely composed of bad features.

I may as well get it over with and tell you what the rest of me's like. So far you've got freckles and thick eyebrows, right? OK, add to that frizzy blondish-red hair that sticks out as far as it goes downwards, a big mouth (in more than one way) and eyes which are a boring sort of grey-green colour, and you've got the complete picture.

Now for a big contrast. Leah Bryan, the musician, is not only the most talented of us all because she plays the violin and the piano to a really high standard, she's also one of those pale, interesting people with long fine blonde hair, and skin that's all creamy and flawless. But – get this – she spends her entire life worrying about things! If I looked like her I'd spend all my time strolling about on cloud forty-nine, surveying the lesser mortals below.

Leah's best friend is Andy, the daring one. Andy's really called Agnès Sorrell. You pronounce Agnès, Ann-yes, because she's half French and has a French name. We all just say Andy, though. Her mum is French and her dad is English. Her dad is also really scary. The others are all petrified of him, even Andy herself. My one big claim to fame is that Andy's dad does not scare me in the least! I don't know why. It's just one of those things. Andy is the smallest of us all with very short dark hair and dark eyes.

Right now I'd give anything to be the same size as Andy, because then I'd get away with joining the junior drama group and landing the main part in their production of the musical *Annie*.

Let me explain. I go to drama club every week because acting is my number one love. The teacher is called Sally Ahlers and she's brilliant. I'm in the twelve-to-fifteens class, but the eight-to-elevens are about to put on *Annie*, and that's my very favourite musical in the world. I know all the songs and practically every word Annie has to say. Anyway, I asked Megan, one of the girls who goes to the eight-to-elevens, to ask Sally if I'd be allowed to audition for the part. Well, this morning at break, she came back with Sally's answer. I've done nothing but think about what she said all day, and right now I'm feeling totally miserable and rather cross about it, because this is what Sally apparently said: "I can't be having great gallumphing thirteen-year-olds on the stage surrounded by little squidgy eight- and nine-year-olds. Tell Lucy she'll be far better off in her own class in her own production."

The more I think about it the more depressed I feel, because unless I magically shrink I'll never get the chance to be Annie in any production *ever*!

4

On top of that there's this dog that keeps following me. It's got hair that's much the same as mine – thick, curly and of no definable colour. I can hardly see his eyes under his great shaggy mane, but I'd bet my bottom dollar they're green, and quite honestly it wouldn't surprise me to find a smattering of freckles on his face.

It started about ten minutes ago, this game of doggy detectives. I was walking down to the café from school, not because it was my turn to work, but just because I felt like joining the others for a short time to give me some strength for tackling my homework – or, to put it another way, to get the answers to my French off Jaimini or Andy.

Anyway, I was on my own because the French teacher, Mr Drop Dead Gorgeous Manson, had kept me back to go over the *passé composé*. Unfortunately, I didn't take in a single word he said because I was too entranced by his wonderful eyes. I was also very engrossed in trying to work out the very youngest age he could be, to see if there might just be a remote chance of him fancying me.

I had put a great deal of effort into arranging myself as gracefully and sexily as possible, and I'd also done a lot of stuff with my eyes that I'd read in a magazine was guaranteed to attract *any* man you wanted. At one point I'd very nearly gone cross-eyed with the effort, but Macho Manson didn't even notice, which only served to plunge me even further into the depths of despair. Clearly I was too old and *far* too big to be Annie, but I was too young and obviously not attractive enough for anyone to fancy me.

To be honest, I didn't really care all that much about Macho Manson, but I *did* care about having the role of Annie, and I couldn't get Sally's words out of my head... "Great galumphing thirteen-year-olds" indeed! I looked down and kicked a stone aggressively, and that was when I suddenly became aware of the hairy hound.

"Hello, Hairy," I remarked, in my voice for dogs, but he didn't answer so I pulled out a savoury scone from my packed lunchbox and dropped it. Normally I wouldn't be that generous with my savoury scones, especially to a dog, because it has to be said that I'm not exactly the world's greatest dog lover, but as I'd only put half the proper quantity of cheese into the scones by mistake, they tasted like nothing, really.

In no time at all, the hairy hound was walking at my side, just as though we were mistress and dog going for our regular walkies. I bent down and looked at the name on his collar but there wasn't one, so I decided to stick with Hairy, and I gave him another scone. I had no problem with him until I got into Cableden High Street and then I began to feel just the teensiest bit anxious.

There was a notice in the café window that read SORRY, NO DOGS, and I wasn't sure that Hairy could read, which meant that it would be up to me to be totally brutal and desert him. This didn't worry me one iota, but something told me that Hairy might take it personally.

Sure enough, outside the café door, he stuck like glue to my side and began wagging his tail as if to say, "Great idea, Luce, I *was* feeling rather peckish, I must admit." I peered through the glass to try and attract Jaimini's attention, but for once, not one of my friends was staring around. They were all engrossed in talking.

I bent down and gave Hairy a quick pat, which was my way of saying, "Bye, mate, nice knowing you, but here endeth our brief relationship," then I quickly opened the door and tried to bolt inside and shut it again before he could follow me. I hadn't bargained for his lightning get-through-doors technique, though, and even though I was as fast as it was humanly possible to be, Hairy finished up inside the café with me.

This, of course, had the instant effect of attracting the attention of not only Jaimini and the others, but also of Jan and Becky. Becky also works there, by the way. Of course, every customer in the place was staring in my direction too. I saw one woman immediately jabbing her finger in the air in the vague direction of the "dog" notice, obviously keen to explain to her friends that I was breaking the rules.

· "He won't leave me alone," I said to Jan, before she could start telling me off.

"He's so sweet," Tash said, dropping into a crouched position and stroking Hairy. The others gathered round, except Andy, who's never been very interested in dogs, and Fen, who was presumably in the kitchen, washing up or something.

"I'm sorry, girls, but you know as well as I do that dogs aren't allowed in here. You're not setting a very good example, Lucy," said Jan. "Where did he come from?"

"I've no idea. He just suddenly appeared as I was walking here from school."

Jan did a bit of tut-tutting, then grabbed Hairy by the collar and tried to drag him towards the door. "He can't stay in here, Luce. I'll put him outside and I expect he'll get the message and go off home."

I have to admit I wasn't quite so convinced, because Hairy had somehow managed to wedge himself between my legs and was resisting Jan's tugs as though his life depended upon it.

"Let go of him, Luce," snapped Jan, but softly because of the customers.

"I'm not holding on to him," I protested, trying to get out of Hairy's clutches, and plunging into the chair next to Andy. "Believe me, I'm as keen to get shot of him as you are."

With the help of Becky, Jan managed to drag the poor beast outside, then they both got back to work. Our table, along with one or two other tables, couldn't help throwing glances at the door, though, because every so often the top of Hairy's head would appear imploringly at the glass panel in the upper half of the door.

Tash, Leah and Jaimini couldn't stop going on and on about him, while Andy and I rolled our eyes at each other because we both thought they were completely bonkers to be so interested in a dog!

"Oh, look, Leah," Tash said, pushing her lips forwards in that sort of kissy expression that people reserve for pets and babies and things. "He's so sweet and cuddly. I wish I could take him home."

"Your mum might not react quite so well to a second dog as she did to the first one," Leah pointed out gently, because Tash had gone home with this puppy called Boo one day without asking her mum or anything, but fortunately her mum had been really touched.

"What are you going to do if he's still out there when we go?" Jaimini asked me.

"What am *I* going to do! Why me? He's not *my* responsibility, you know!" I pointed out, rather snappily, only because I was still upset about what Sally had said.

"Well, somebody's got to do something, haven't they? We can't just leave him there," Jaimini replied.

"Let's cross that bridge when we come to it, shall we?" I said, scanning the rest of the people in the café because I was bored with the conversation. "Oh, by the way, Andy, could you help me with my Fren—"

I stopped suddenly because I had been rendered speechless by the sight of the most amazing guy I had ever set eyes on. Yes, I know what you must be thinking, but I'm not really that bad, honestly.

"What's the matter now, Luce?" asked Jaimini, turning round to see what had struck me dumb. As soon as she'd seen, she whizzed back round again, and ordered me to stop staring. "Honestly, Luce, I can't take you anywhere!"

"I thought you were head over heels in love with your French teacher," Andy commented, calmly.

"Not any more," I breathed, trying to steal a look at Mr Amazing without Jaimini noticing.

"You're crazy, Luce," said Leah, shaking her head with a little smile.

"Tell me something new," said Fen, appearing at our table. "Want a drink, Luce?"

I didn't answer because I was otherwise engaged.

"Get her a Coke and stick some anti-male agent in it," advised Andy, the wit.

"I can't help it," I told them. "I'm just more mature than you lot."

They laughed at that. Typical! I ignored them. But then I nearly fainted because that spectacularly amazing guy, who couldn't have been more than twenty-two – OK, twenty-five – actually smiled at me. Not at one of the others, but at me! Double wow!

"He smiled at me," I squeaked out of the corner of my mouth.

"He probably thinks he must know you because you're gawping at him," Fen hissed, leaning forwards.

"Stop drooling, Luce, for goodness' sake," Jaimini added.

"He's going," I told them, breathlessly.

"Well, isn't that just the most unexpected behaviour you've ever come across?" commented Andy sarcastically, turning to Fen.

I watched him as discreetly as possible as he paid Becky at the counter, then strolled out of the café. He bent down just outside the door, then, after a few seconds, straightened up again and set off along the High Street.

"I think I'll follow him," I announced.

"No, you will not," five voices informed me in unison.

"Why not?" I whined.

"Because he's far too old for you," Jaimini told me.

"Why can't you like boys of your own age?" Fen asked.

"I've told you, I'm too mature."

There was more eye-rolling after I said that, then I just sat quietly, day-dreaming about him while the others got on with their own conversations. I was aware of Jaimini casting worried looks in my direction, but I tried to ignore them because they were interrupting my lovely thoughts.

When I'd played through every possible day-dream of *him* and me together at a disco, at a restaurant, at a dance, on a Greek island, I felt the need to talk about him so I leaned forwards and asked the others how old they thought he was and what they guessed his job was.

"Oh, she's returned from her travels," commented Andy, not realizing how true her words were. Fen had gone back to work by then, and I was glad because that made one less cynic in the group.

"I guess he's about ... mm, let me see ... fifty-three in the shade," joked Jaimini, which made me hit her. It was only a tap but she acted as though I'd given her a right hook or something.

"No need to be so aggressive, Luce. I thought you were supposed to be mature!"

"OK, forget his age, what about his job?"

"Well, let's see, what was he wearing?" Andy answered me. "Faded blue jeans, T-shirt, dirty trainers, tatty jacket… I'd say he was probably the financial director of a large and flourishing company somewhere in the City. What do you think, Tash?"

"Don't bother to tell me, if you're not going to be serious," I warned Tash.

"I guess he's a male nurse," Tash said, unexpectedly.

"Yes, or a writer," Leah added, looking thoughtful.

"Something compassionate…" Tash went on.

"Or artistic," Leah added.

I eyed them carefully to check they weren't mucking about, but they weren't, and I felt heartened that they obviously thought he was a nice guy with a sensitive, caring nature.

"I've got to go," Leah said suddenly, looking at her watch.

"Yeah, me too," added Andy. So we all decided to go then. I wondered briefly whether it would be worth legging it up the High Street to see if I could catch a glimpse of the latest man in my life, but I decided it would be a waste of time, and I just prayed that fate would be kind to me and let me see him again before too long. I would have been over the moon had I guessed just how kind fate was to prove to be!

"Look at this," Tash called out from the bulletin board, where people stick cards about things for sale or whatever.

We crowded round and followed Tash's finger jabbing at the board.

"One, two, three, four, *five* adverts, all with animals for sale. Incredible, isn't it?"

The others all seemed to agree with her and I gave the impression that I agreed too, but actually I'd never been all that interested in animals, so it didn't strike me as particularly incredible.

We said goodbye to Fen and Jan, then went out. Guess who was waiting patiently by the door? Yep, you got it. Hairy! Even though it was Tash and Leah who were bending down and cooing over him, he plonked himself firmly at my side and gave me a bark and a little pitiful cry, which made Tash and Leah more gooey and besotted than ever.

"Oh, Luce, he loves you. Look!"

"You'll have to take him home with you and ask your mum what to do," advised Jaimini.

"OK," I said, rather grumpily. My sudden bad mood wasn't anything to do with what Jaimini had said. It was because when Leah had stood up straight, she'd tossed her long hair casually over her shoulder and readjusted her school bag, and I'd noticed how lovely and slim she was, and all with no effort at all. I'd often noticed how slim she was, of course, but this time it sort of hit me between the eyes. I glanced down at myself and felt so clumsy and unattractive. Then, worst of all, I caught sight of my reflection in the café window. I was standing next to Andy, and she looked like Miss Petite, whereas I looked like Miss Clodhopper.

So, Sally had been right. I was big. I was *gallumphing*. If I'd looked like Andy or even Leah, who was only an inch or so smaller than me, I probably would have been considered for the part of Annie. Life wasn't fair. It really wasn't.

"Seeya," I called, striding off, trying to look nonchalant, so no one would know how screwed up I was feeling inside.

"See you tomorrow, Luce," Jaimini called, an unmistakable note of concern in her voice. She knows me well, does Jaimini, and she knew I was hacked off, but probably didn't think that a dog was enough to have that effect on me. Although it's very nice and comforting in one way to have caring friends like that, in another way it can be a bit of a drag, because you have to work extra hard if you want to keep anything secret from them.

When I got home, Mum was in the kitchen surrounded by pots and pans and dishes and plates of food, food, food. She works as a free-lance caterer and she was in the middle of a job for someone. I thought the food smelt awful. Hairy, on the other hand, thought he'd died and gone to heaven. Ignoring my shouts, he positively galloped into the kitchen.

"Hairy! No! Get down! Bad dog!"

"What the…!" began Mum, her eyes widening in horror as one of her beef casseroles hit the floor and at least half of it went before I could pull the stupid dog off it.

"Get that thing out of here!" Mum exploded, when she'd regained the power of speech.

"I'm trying to," I replied, yanking on the stupid dog's collar for dear life.

"Where on earth…?" she went on, pushing Hairy's bottom vigorously but getting nowhere.

At that point the twins came in. Leo and Tim are my eight-year-old half-brothers. They're not best known for their sensitivity and tact.

"Oh, great! A dog! Can we keep him?" was Leo's immediate response.

"He's hungry, look. Let's give him a bit of this, Mum. You won't miss a little bit, will you?"

"Don't touch anything, Tim. Not *a thing*!" Mum warned them in a frantic voice. She was still wrestling with Hairy, who had managed to break free of both our clutches and was heading for the steak and kidney pie that Tim was holding.

"I said, don't touch… Oh, Tim! You absolute idiot!" she screeched.

Tim, realizing that he'd made a huge mistake, was trying to drag the steak and kidney pie away from Hairy, but it was too late. The dog didn't get as far as eating it but he did headbutt it, which ruined it, of course.

"You stupid idiot, Tim!" I agreed with Mum, as I used every ounce of strength I possessed to manhandle the great gallumphing specimen out of the back door, and shut it firmly behind him.

"What a fiasco!" Mum said, in a dangerously low voice.

"I'm really sorry, Mum, but I don't know what on earth to do with him. He just followed me to the café, and Jan forced him out. Then I found him still waiting for me when we left later. Jaimini said I ought to bring him home and ask you what to do."

"Well, I've got a few good suggestions, I can tell you," murmured Mum, through tight lips. "Number one, the police. What's his name?" She was already at the phone.

"No idea. It's not on his collar."

"Hello… Directory Enquiries? I need the number of my local police station… Sorry? Cableden… Right, thank you."

She had scribbled down a number which she was already tapping in. I listened vaguely to what

17

she was saying to the local police, while I tried to clear up some of the mess that Hairy had made.

"Can't you help, you two, instead of just standing there!" I snapped, but I regretted saying it because Tim and Leo are not two of the most natural helpers in the world, and if anything they were making an even worse mess.

"Leave that, you two," Mum said with a sigh, as she picked up a cloth. "As soon as it's reported missing, they'll let us know," she said, in answer to my enquiring look.

"And what do we do in the meantime?" I asked.

"They're kind of assuming we'll hang on to it, I think."

"Don't keep calling him 'it', Mum," said Leo, accusingly.

"Yeah, mega! We'll hang on to him, won't we?" Tim asked his twin.

They stood there, trying to look appealing, on their thin little legs. (Oh, why has everybody got such thin legs all of a sudden?)

"We'll go out and play with him in the garden, OK, Mum?"

"Just make sure that it does *not*, on *any* account, come back into this kitchen," Mum warned them, in a voice that meant business.

"Don't worry, he won't," grinned Tim, opening the door about ten centimetres and squeezing his thin little body through the crack. Leo's equally thin little body then slithered out and the door closed behind them.

"What if no one reports him missing by the time we're going to bed, Mum? He can't stay out there tonight."

"Start praying," she told me briefly, as she turned her full attention back to her job.

"I'll do my homework," I told her.

"Good girl," she said, rather absent-mindedly, so I went upstairs.

In my bedroom, I sat on my bed, feeling worse than I'd felt all day. After a minute I got up and stood in front of my full length mirror and looked at myself from every possible angle. I grabbed hold of my hair with both hands and pressed it flat against my head. As soon as I let go, it sprang back up to its stupid sticking-out position, so I wet it, knowing that I was only temporarily curing the problem. Next, I took off everything except my underwear and scrutinized myself again from every angle.

"I hate you," I told my reflection, softly. "And I'm going to get rid of you," I added.

It was funny, but as I said that, I could feel a sort of power running through my blood. This was the answer to all my problems. I just needed to be thin and nonchalant like Leah – or even *very* thin like Fen – and I'd be so much more attractive. After all, Leah had Oliver, and Fen had

Matthew. That proved it.

"We'll eat in about twenty minutes, OK?" Mum called up the stairs.

"OK," I called back.

"*You* might eat, but I won't," I added, under my breath.

Chapter 2

By nine o'clock that evening it had become perfectly obvious that Hairy was not about to go away and leave us all alone. Terry, my stepdad, had come home, and thought it was great to have a dog. He couldn't understand what the fuss was about.

"The fuss is because the stupid animal managed to wolf his way through half a beef casserole and half a steak and kidney pie, which were pretty much my profit margin for this job," Mum replied, folding her arms and giving Terry an "answer that!" look.

"Well, clout him next time," was Terry's lighthearted response.

"There won't *be* a next time," Mum replied.

"Shall I ring Tash or Leah, Mum?" I asked. "They both thought Hairy was really sweet. I reckon Jaimini wouldn't mind looking after him for a while either, but her parents would definitely say no."

At that point the phone had rung. It was old Mrs Stone, who lives next door but one. She was phoning about some poetry competition that she'd seen in a magazine, wondering if Mum wanted to enter it. Mum nattered for a bit, and along the way she told Mrs Stone about Hairy. It's not always easy following one-sided conversations, but this one soon became crystal clear, if the look on Mum's face was anything to go by.

"Really? I'd not idea you were so fond of... Well, what a coincidence... No, not at all. Quite the opposite, in fact... No, it's not that we don't like dogs, it's just that this one seems fairly boisterous... Well, why don't you come round and have a look? You might not like him... Um... Hairy... Yes, I know it's an odd name. It was Lucy who gave him the name... Incidentally, the dog is very struck on Lucy. It followed her to the café from school, then waited outside the café and followed her home... Yes... All right... See you in a minute."

"She wants to take him?" I asked, happily.

"Well, she heard him barking when she was in her garden. And you know Mrs Stone, she couldn't resist finding out where he came from. Apparently she's been debating whether to get another dog ever since her old one died."

Only the twins looked downcast. "You're cruel, you are," was Tim's summary of our behaviour.

"And I'm going to report you to the NSPCC, I am," Leo added.

"You might find the RSPCA showing a little more interest," Terry advised, with a quick wink at me. Then we all stayed quiet because Mrs Stone's footsteps could clearly be heard coming round the back. Her first glimpse of Hairy couldn't have been better timed. He was lying down and staring with big soulful eyes at Mrs Stone as she approached. She seemed bowled over, which was surprising because Hairy didn't wag his tail or move any other part of himself for that matter.

"He's adorable," she said, bending over with a straight back in the very sturdy, feet-apart way that old ladies have. "Aren't you, hmm?"

She began vigorously stroking him, while nodding and keeping up a continuous patter. I don't know why, but I've always found it really weird when people talk to dogs as though they're people, and I could feel a bubble of laughter starting somewhere deep inside me.

"Well, you're welcome to keep him," Mum said. "But what if you get attached to him and the owners turn up and want him back? It's pretty likely, I would have thought."

"I'll just have to hand him over," said Mrs Stone, with a sigh.

With that she whipped a lead out of her pocket and nimbly fixed it to Hairy's collar. "Come on, Kenneth, we're away to my house, old boy."

"Kenneth!" I nearly exploded.

"Ssh," Mum cautioned me with a flap of her hand, but I could see she was cracking up, too. We waited till Mrs Stone had gone striding off with her new charge, calling out that she'd contact the police to let them know the latest development, then we all burst out laughing.

"Fancy calling a dog *Kenneth*," spluttered Terry.

Tim and Leo didn't think it was at all funny, but then they always make a point of disagreeing with what everybody else thinks. It's just one of their irritating little habits.

That night I lay in bed, absolutely starving. I'd hardly touched a thing at dinner time with Mum and Terry and the twins. I'd thought it might be quite difficult to get away with because I usually eat very heartily and I was afraid Mum might think I was sickening for something. I started with as little as possible on my plate, then just pushed the food around, and no one even noticed.

Before going to bed I'd weighed myself. I was eight-stone-one, which was two pounds less than the last time I'd weighed myself. It looked as though my weight-loss campaign was working already.

Lying in bed, I stretched out to make myself as long and thin as possible, then put my hands round my waist and reached my fingers out as far as they would go. At the front my middle fingers were touching and at the back my thumbs were about ten centimetres apart. There and then I made a resolution. I wouldn't give in on my "get thin and attractive" campaign until my thumbs touched. I smiled to myself in the dark. It all seemed so easy.

Then I lay quite still for ages thinking about Mr Amazing – the writer, or maybe the male nurse. I added a career of my own – the actor. That would be the very best thing of all that he could turn out to be, because then we'd have so much in common. Acting is my passion, you see. Also, actors are extremely offbeat people, and it might just turn out that this one wouldn't hold my age against me.

The following morning break, the six of us gathered at our favourite outdoor meeting place down at the netball courts, which are miles away from where most people congregate at break times. I told them all about Hairy, but I wasn't really concentrating on what I was saying because I was trying to sit in exactly the same position as Leah to see whether my arms looked as thin as hers. Next, I studied her legs and felt an instant pang of jealousy that she could look so good. My own legs looked revolting so I stretched them out, which improved matters slightly, but not enough for my liking.

"Do you want to finish these off, Luce?" asked Jaimini, offering me half a packet of Hula Hoops. Normally I would have jumped at the offer and I very nearly did then, out of habit, but I remembered just in time.

"I'm not all that hungry…"

Gasps all round, because everyone knows that Luce will eat anything at *any* time. I felt I needed to offer a bit more explanation.

"I think double cookery has had a bad effect on me," I said, lightly.

Why wasn't anyone saying anything? Surely I couldn't be *that* transparent. There was no way they could know what I was up to, was there?

"We were making fish pie, and Mum's made so many of them lately I think I'll be sick if I have to see or smell another one." I tried to look as casual as possible but I wasn't sure if it was working.

"I hope you're not going on a diet or anything," said Jaimini, carefully.

"Diet? Me? You must be joking!"

As soon as the words were out of my mouth I thought, "Watch out Luce, don't overdo it." My heart was beating faster than usual. I knew why. It was because I'd told a big lie. I had to, though. There was no way I could possibly ever let *anyone* know my plan. It was too personal. I didn't want any of my friends to know I was worrying about being overweight. Also everybody was obsessed by eating disorders these days, which had nothing to do with my plan, so it was important that I kept my slimming scheme to myself or people would worry when there really wasn't any need.

It would be impossible to explain to anyone that I simply wanted to lose a few pounds – well, say a stone at the most – so that I'd look good. I could just hear Mum's concerned voice: "You don't *need* to lose weight, Luce. You're lovely and slim as you are." Well, I knew I wasn't exactly fat, but there was definitely room for improvement, and because of my ridiculous hair and my freckles, it was extra important to have a very slim body. Nobody need ever know what I was doing. I'd just quietly lose the weight, and then revel in everybody's admiring glances.

"Wake up, Luce," Fen was saying.

"Oh, sorry – what?"

"We've got that talk after break, haven't we? You know – from that vet who's coming."

"Oh, yes…"

"You could tell him or her about Hairy, couldn't you?" Leah suggested.

"What, something like this, you mean? 'By the way, Mr Vet, this dog followed me home yesterday, but I can't stand dogs so I let the neighbour have it.'"

The others were half-laughing when I said that, but it was obvious that Tash and Leah didn't approve of my attitude towards animals.

"Anyway, it's better than lessons, isn't it?" said Andy, and there we all agreed.

So at five-past eleven the whole of years seven, eight and nine were packed into the assembly hall awaiting the great vet. It was surprising how many people were really excited about the talk and had got lots of questions to ask at the end. Tash had said she wouldn't mind being a vet when she grew up, and I could easily imagine her in that role, actually. I'm going to be an actress, of course – a very thin one.

I glanced round and noticed with satisfaction that Ellie Cooper was looking fairly chubby and so was Susanne Hamton, who was sitting next to Ellie. It's funny how fat people are drawn towards each other, I thought, casting my eye round the big hall. At the other side there were two other plump-looking girls from year nine, who I didn't know, also sitting together. I looked down at myself and felt a nice little thrill of satisfaction that at least my problem wasn't too big to overcome.

I'd had very little breakfast but Mum had been watching me, so I'd had to have half a piece of toast. She'd made me some cocoa but I'd only drunk about three mouthfuls, then tipped it down the sink when she wasn't looking. Milk has got quite a lot of calories in it, you see.

I could hear Ms Chambers' footsteps coming down the hall. She's our headteacher. I didn't bother to turn round because it was more interesting looking at Jaimini's outstretched arm. Her sleeve was rolled up and her hand was clutching the back of the chair in front of us. Like everyone else Jaimini was engrossed in craning round to see the vet, so I subtly rolled up my own sleeve, then stretched out my arm in the same position as Jaimini's so that I could compare the size and shape. What I saw did *not* fill me with glee. Jaimini's arm was definitely thinner, and because her skin is so dark it looked even more slender. That jealousy thing hit me hard in the stomach, and I had to bite my tongue not to snap at poor Jaimes when she started saying excitedly, "Look who it is, look who it is, Luce!"

Trying to look enthusiastic, I sat up straight and craned my neck to see over the heads of the girls in front of us. What I saw made every fibre in my body spring to attention. There, standing at the front, smiling and wonderful in a dark blue shirt and a pair of black jeans, stood *Mr Amazing*!

"I'd like to introduce you all to Steve Rogers, who, as you know, is a vet," announced the very smiley Ms Chambers. She turned towards him for a moment. "We've all been greatly looking forward to your visit, Mr Rogers, so without further ado I'm going to hand straight over to you."

Ms Chambers began the clapping and we, the audience, joined in enthusiastically. It's not always like this when we have visitors to the school. The clapping would be very thin if it was an accountant in a suit who'd come to give us the benefit of his business.

"Steve, a vet!" I whispered under my breath. Thank goodness I'd looked at him for so long in the café, because otherwise he'd never have smiled at me. So when I went up to him at the end of this talk, he'd be sure to recognize me, and if there were tons of students wanting to talk to him, he'd be much more likely to pick me.

The whole auditorium was silent, waiting to hear what he was like. I glanced round to see what effect he was having on the other girls. Tash's face was the first I saw. She just looked normal. But that was because Tash was genuinely very interested in what the vet had to say. I tried to imitate her attentive expression. After all, if I was to get closer to Steve I needed to develop an interest in his subject.

"Good morning, everybody, and thank you very much for such an enthusiastic welcome. Can I ask first of all, how many of you have got pets at home?"

Over half the hands went up, including mine.

Andy and Jaimini both immediately gave me "What a cheek!" looks, and Andy hissed, "Hairy's not exactly yours, Luce!"

"Don't split hairs," I replied, without taking my eyes off Steve.

Andy laughed at that, and so did the others. I felt glad that they were all back to thinking "Here's Luce, true to form, fancying an older, totally unsuitable person." It kept their minds off the biggest thing on *my* mind, which was the new me I was creating.

Steve's talk was quite interesting, I suppose, if you're passionate about animals, and the video he showed was certainly gripping, but apart from the fact that it was excellent missing lessons, I wasn't about to become a born-again animal lover.

After an hour and ten minutes it was question time. I had decided not to ask a question at this point because I didn't want to get caught up with all the others. I wanted my question to stand out, so I'd decided to leave it till most of the students had drifted away, and catch Steve at the front as he was packing his things away. Tash's hand was stretched up high, and so was Fen's. Steve seemed to be looking at Fen.

"Yes, the girl with the brown hair…"

Fen was sitting next to me. She wasn't sure if Steve meant her. She was looking round to check.

"Yes, that's right, you… Sitting next to the girl with the blonde curly hair."

My heart leapt. *Blonde, curly hair!* Not red, frizzy hair! I smiled at him, then felt stupid because he wasn't even looking at me, he was listening to Fen who was going on about her rabbit, Bracken. I suddenly remembered something that my dad – my *real* dad, I mean – once told me. He was quoting a vet friend of his who had said that rabbits weren't particularly good pets because they were thick, smelly and dirty, whereas rats were excellent pets because they got on really well with humans, they were clean and they were intelligent. An idea was forming in my mind. I would blind Steve with science. Yes, I would demonstrate my great understanding of animals, and then go on to ask his advice about Hairy. I'd pretend I'd still got him. In fact, I could invent an illness for Hairy and even arrange to take him to Steve's surgery.

Fen's question had been answered and Steve was talking to one of the boys about his Russian hamster and how you could tell what sex it was. It was Paul Tyman who'd asked the question, and judging from the way the boys around him were all sniggering, he'd only asked it for a laugh. I looked at Steve. He obviously hadn't realized. He was banging on about gestation – whatever that was! It slightly irritated me that Steve hadn't even worked out what the boys were up to, but I forgave him because he was so devastatingly gorgeous.

I kept on wishing Steve would wind it up because I didn't want Leah to get her question answered and she kept on shooting her hand up so vigorously that Steve was bound to ask her next. Sure enough, he did. I stared at him really hard when he was listening to Leah. I'm sure I wasn't mistaken, Steve obviously thought Leah was lovely. Who wouldn't? It made me sick, and for a moment I felt this feeling of utter despair, because however slim I got, I couldn't make my hair lose weight, could I?

At last Ms Chambers got up and thanked Mr Rogers for "such an informative and tremendously enjoyable morning" and the students made a rush for the door. It was lunch time and everybody wanted to get into the queue first. The people who had packed lunches weren't in all that much of a hurry, though. Fen, Tash and Leah stood up, chatting excitedly to each other about it all. They drifted out with the others, not paying attention to what Jaimini, Andy and I were doing. Andy said she'd got a running practice and went off on her own. I could tell she needed to stretch her legs and get moving after all that sitting still, because Andy's always like that.

"Coming, Luce?" said Jaimini.

"You go on, Jaimes. I'm just going to quickly ask him about Hairy. He might even know whose dog it is, you never know."

"That's a good idea, Luce," she said. "I knew you cared about the poor dog underneath." She grinned at me. "Or is it the vet you care about?"

"Well, you know, a bit of both," I said, lightly.

She tut-tutted a bit, then said she'd get my packed lunch and see me in a minute on the netball courts.

"Yeah, seeya!"

Good. Here was my chance at last. I pulled hard on my stomach muscles, made my shoulders square like Tash's and tried to walk like Leah does, with a sort of saunter. I needn't have bothered. Steve was bending down with his back to me, fiddling with the video machine. Mrs Williams was stacking up chairs with a couple of other teachers and the last remaining students.

"Steve," I murmured.

He turned round and shot up with a startled look in his eyes which immediately changed to a smile of recognition.

"Hi!"

"Hi, I'm Lucy Edmunson. I saw you the other day in the café, and I just wondered whether you happened to notice the dog that was outside the door?" I tipped my head to one side, then quickly straightened it because I couldn't concentrate on holding my stomach in when I'd got my head on the side, for some unknown reason. (I made a mental note to practise coordination exercises.)

"Yes… Yes, I did. I *did*. Yes."

Good. I'd got him really interested.

"Well, that dog followed me from school to the café, and then he waited outside for me and followed me all the way home." I smiled a slow smile without letting my teeth show because I thought it would look more appealing.

"So, let me get this straight. You'd never seen the dog before, you mean?"

"No, and I was wondering whether by some miracle, you might just happen to know whose it is?"

"No, I don't… Was there no name or anything on the collar?"

"Nothing."

"Have you contacted the police?"

"Yes, I have."

"Well, there's nothing more you can do. You must have got some special animal magnetism, Lucy. Some people have, you know."

I gave him another of my slow smiles because I reckoned the other one went down pretty well. And then another idea took root. Steve had given me the perfect cue.

"I've had that said to me before," I improvized, with a sort of modest look.

35

"Really?"

"Yes, but I'm sure I haven't got anything special…"

"You're too modest, Lucy."

This time he smiled at *me*, and my heart, along with various other vital organs, all melted.

"Somebody said I was – you know – sort of *psychic* where animals were concerned, but I'm sure they didn't know what they were talking about."

"Who was it who said that?" he asked with a frown and I knew I'd really got him interested. I also knew I was going to regret going on like this. A little voice inside me was saying, "Shut up, Luce! Just say you're worried about Hairy, make the appointment and *go*!" but I couldn't. It was as though my voice wasn't my own.

"He was a vet too, actually."

"Well, there must be some sort of truth in it, then."

"Well, I don't know." I tried to look as though I found my incredible skill rather embarrassing. "But I was going to ask you, um, Steve… Could I bring Hair…" I couldn't call him Hairy, that would just make the whole thing seem ridiculous. On the other hand, he might think that was very original of me. "I call him Hairy… I know it's stupid…"

He laughed at that. "No, it's not. It's great!"

"Anyway, could I bring him to see you, because I think I can sort of sense that he's suffering, even though there aren't any real symptoms."

"Yes, of course." He dug into his pocket and pulled out a card. "Here you are. Ring up and make an appointment. What other pets have you got, by the way?"

"Just my rat – Zonc," I told him, glibly. Goodness knows where I got the name Zonc from. It was just the first thing that popped into my head.

"A rat! That's quite unusual for a girl."

I knew I'd been smart saying I'd got a rat, and now I was going to really impress him. If I concentrated I could spout the exact words that my dad had said the vet had said.

"Yeah, I know, but rats are so much more intelligent than say, er, rabbits. They interact with humans and they're so clean. Personally I don't see the point of owning a dirty, smelly, thick rabbit." I opened my eyes wide and held his gaze. A lovely feeling was spreading over me because I could tell Steve thought I was totally original and interesting.

"Well, I must say it's very refreshing to hear someone as young as you who really knows what they're talking about," he praised me.

I was positively glowing by then but I needed to wind the conversation up because there was no way I could hold my stomach in for another second, and my cheeks were aching with the effort of trying to keep them sucked in all the time. Never mind, I wouldn't have to work so hard at trying to look thin and lovely for much longer because soon I *really* would be.

He looked at his watch and started rushing then. "I must get going or I'll be late for my next appointment."

"I'll see you soon then ... with Hairy," I smiled, then I quickly turned and walked off with the hint of a wiggle, like I'd seen Leah do. (Only she did it naturally, like everything else, lucky thing.)

"You've been ages," began Jaimini accusingly, when I sat down with her at the netball courts a few minutes later.

"I've been discussing Hairy," I told her, briefly. "I'm starving."

"Here you are." She handed me my packed lunch and I opened it, feeling ravenous. Then as I set eyes on the sandwiches I remembered with horror that I'd completely forgotten about my diet. Never mind. It didn't matter that I'd said I was starving. In fact, it made it better in a way. I had rehearsed what I was about to do in front of the mirror that morning, but I still felt nervous about actually carrying it out. I picked up one of the sandwiches and, when I was about to take a bite, I stopped dramatically and began sniffing it and frowning.

"Oh, no! I don't believe it!"

"What?" Jaimini asked me, full of concern.

"I've only gone and put the wrong sandwich spread in it. Yuk! Smell that!"

I thrust the sandwich under her nose.

"Yuk!" she agreed. "It smells of old fish! How ever did you manage to do that, Luce? You don't normally have things that have gone off in your house."

"It's my fault. I noticed it was going off ages ago and kept meaning to chuck it away, but never quite did. Mum wouldn't notice because she never goes into that bit of the cupboard."

What I'd actually done was to leave a small tin of tuna that was on its last legs out all night, then mixed a bit of it into the sandwich spread on my sandwiches.

"Oh, Luce, and I've finished all my sandwiches, otherwise you could have shared mine."

"It doesn't matter. I had a huge breakfast and I expect I'll stuff myself when I get home from school. I'll just eat this apple that mum insisted I put in."

Jaimini seemed to accept that all right, and I ate my apple as slowly as I could because the hunger pangs were so awful I could hardly bear them. I began to weaken. I was on duty at the café after school. I daydreamed about having a huge burger and chips, but then I looked at Jaimini, who had lain back on the grass next to the netball courts because the sun was nice and hot. She looked like a model or something. The same jealous pang pierced me and brought back my resolution to be thin – in fact, the thinnest of us all.

Chapter 3

At four o'clock I went in through the back door to the kitchen of the café to find Kevin, the chef, singing away. Kevin, who's twenty-one, is about fourth on my list of gorgeous guys. You should see him. He's small and wiry and very strong. Actually, he's dropped down to fifth place now that Steve has appeared on the scene.

"Hiya, Luce! How's tricks?" he asked, without even looking in my direction.

"How did you know it was me?" I challenged him. "You haven't learnt the rota off by heart, have you?"

"I always get this funny feeling when it's you," he answered. "It's like a premonition that trouble's just arrived."

"Get lost," I said, punching his arm, but not too hard.

"Hello, Luce," Jan said, coming through from

the café with a full tray which she handed straight to me. "Perfect timing. Dishwasher, please."

I noticed that there was a sausage roll that hadn't been touched on the top plate, and the temptation to eat it was almost unbearable. I put the tray down, checked that neither Jan nor Kevin was looking, then put my hands round my waist while breathing right in, to see if the gap between my thumbs had narrowed at all. I thought it probably had, which made me feel a little wave of happiness. I knew I'd have to eat something at home but I thought I'd try and make it as little as possible, and hope that Mum had done plenty of vegetables because there aren't many calories in vegetables.

In fact, perhaps it would be a good idea to eat a carrot there and then. I quickly loaded up the dishwasher, then Kevin asked me to wash some pans for him. By then I was absolutely desperate to eat something, but it would be far too time-wasting to peel a carrot, so I quickly stuffed the whole sausage roll into my mouth and devoured it greedily, thinking thank goodness I hadn't got round to putting it into the bin.

When I'd done the washing-up, I went through to the café and was immediately beckoned over by the others.

"Look, Luce, we've got you a present," Jaimini announced, and there on a plate was another sausage roll, two polo mints, half a piece of chocolate cake, half a piece of toast and three fruit pastilles.

"We've saved our last morsels for our poor, starving friend. Aren't we good?" Tash said, brightly, and I looked round at their grinning faces.

"Well, don't thank us, will you?" said Jaimini, jokingly.

"Oh, yeah, thanks."

I managed a smile then scooped up the plate and assured them I'd eat it in the kitchen.

"Go on, then. Off you go. You must be absolutely famished," Fen said.

"Yeah, famished," I agreed, thinking how hard it was going to be resisting this plateful of goodies once I was back in the kitchen. On the other hand if I *did* resist it, I'd feel so guilty that I'd chucked away what my friends had saved specially for me.

I was just turning to go when I heard a familiar voice at the next table.

"Hello, Lucy. Didn't know you worked here."

It was Steve.

"Wondered when you'd notice," Andy said, in a stage whisper, and I could sense the others all stifling their giggles, even though I had my back to them. I presumed they were giggling because next to Steve sat the most glamorous girl I'd ever seen. Her hair was very short and blonde and straight, cut in a sort of modern wedged style. Her eyes were big and blue and her cheekbones were very prominent. The suit she was wearing looked pretty expensive, I can tell you. She was smiling at me, so not only was she beautiful, she was nice. Trust Steve!

"This is Donna Parker," Steve introduced me. "This is Lucy. She was at the school where I did the talk this morning," he went on.

"Hello, Lucy. Pleased to meet you," said Donna, making me feel about as sophisticated as a six-and-a-half-year-old.

"How's that rat of yours? What's his name? Zonc?" asked Steve, in a voice that was practically loud enough for the whole café to hear, but *definitely* loud enough to have reached Jaimini and the others. I felt a blush creeping up from my neck.

"He's OK," I mumbled. "I'd better get back to work," I added quickly, before Steve could carry on. If we left it there, there was a tiny chance that I could make out to the others that they'd all misheard, and Steve had actually said something entirely different. But I was out of luck.

"Lucy's got a real affinity with animals, haven't you?" Steve rattled on while I frantically tried to block the others' view by placing myself right in front of him, in the desperate hope that his voice might not carry so much.

"Tell Donna what you were telling me, Lucy…" He turned to Donna. "Wait till you hear this. This'll really interest you." He turned back to me. "Donna's absolutely potty about all animals. She puts them on a level with human beings. On top of that she's studying applied psychology…" He turned to Donna. "You're going to want to see a demonstration, I'll bet," he went on, cheerfully, while my heart sank nearer and nearer to the ground. Steve was obviously one of those people who like challenges, I thought, heavily. The challenge here was to try and find a common link between a sophisticated, beautiful woman of the world and a stupid school girl with a pathetic craze for rats. "Go on, Lucy, tell Donna."

I leaned forward and spoke in scarcely more than a whisper so that the others wouldn't be able to hear what I was saying. I could tell from the silence behind me that their ears were flapping like mad. I hoped that I was giving Steve and Donna the impression that I was talking softly because I was very modest about my special gift.

"It's nothing much, really. It's just that I can sense what animals are feeling – like if they're unhappy or ill or something. And then I can often cure them."

"Sense if they're ill! Cure them! That's brilliant!" exclaimed Donna, loudly and joyfully.

I wanted to tell her to keep her voice down but obviously I couldn't do that. There was definitely a little explosive noise from the table behind me. I guessed it was Fen cracking up at my expense. My pink face got pinker.

"Well, seriously Lucy, I'd love to see this in action, but I can tell you're really busy right now, so…"

"Yes, I'd better not stand around chatting any longer," I said, thinking immediately that that was a particularly stupid thing to say.

When I'd just about reached the kitchen door, Steve called out, "Be thinking when you can give us a demo, Lucy. Donna's dying to meet Zonc – we both are."

I could have died, especially when I heard the stifled laughter from Fen's table.

"Yeah, OK," I called back, with something that was supposed to be an enthusiastic smile on my face but probably looked more like a demented leer. I shot into the safety of the kitchen where I went straight to the bin and scraped the contents of the plate into it before I could change my mind.

The next second I froze because the door had opened and there stood Jaimini. She froze, too. Her big eyes looked accusingly at the bin as if it had snatched the food from the plate and gobbled it up without consulting me. Our eyes met.

46

"Oh, silly me! Aren't I stupid? I wasn't think-ing," I gabbled, with amazing presence of mind. I was doing my utmost to look really disappointed and it must have been convincing because Jaimini's expression immediately started to match mine, as though she was really cheesed off on my behalf.

"Oh, Luce! Oh, no!" she wailed. But being a positive sort of person, Jaimini was determined that I should eat. So she marched up to Kevin and asked him if she could pinch a few chips from his big trayful.

"Yeah, go ahead," he replied, so I watched in horror as Jaimini got a plate and piled it high with chips, then presented them to me with a big beam on her face. I thought she'd disappear then but she didn't. She just stood there waiting for me to get scoffing. I picked up a chip and started blowing on it as though it was boiling hot – anything to put off having to eat.

"What did you want, anyway?" I asked.

"Oh, yes, we all want to know what you're up to now, Luce," Jaimini said, with a giggle. "Honestly, all that stuff about an imaginary rat called Zonc. You really are a nutter, you know."

I put the chip in my mouth and ate it very slowly. "I have to agree with you I'm afraid, Jaimes," I confessed, because suddenly it didn't seem to matter very much what the others thought about me inventing pet rats to make an impression on the lovely local vet. In a way it was the very diversion I needed to keep their minds off the much more important subject of my diet.

I gave Jaimini a cheeky grin. "I must be stark raving bonkers, mustn't I? It's just that Steve is so gorgeous. I mean, how was I to know that he'd have a girlfriend who's in love with animals and is studying psychology?"

Jaimini laughed, then frowned. "You don't seem very bothered about the girlfriend, Luce."

"No, I'm not," I told her, which was the truth. I knew I couldn't expect Steve to show any interest in me all the time I looked like I did, but I was pretty confident that when the new skinny me emerged he'd be much keener. Meanwhile I had to be as original and interesting as possible. Jaimini was waiting for a bit more explanation, I could tell.

"Be realistic, Jaimes, I can't expect to be his exclusive, one and only girlfriend, can I?"

She just laughed when I said that, which annoyed me because I thought I was showing a great deal of maturity with an attitude like that.

"I'd better get on," I said, turning to the sink.

"Yeah, OK, and you'd better get yourself a rat, too," Jaimini dropped in casually, as though she was just reminding me to do the maths home-work or something.

"Do you think I ought to?" I asked her.

"Well, you'll look pretty silly if Donna turns up on your doorstep one day wanting to meet Zonc, won't you?" laughed Jaimini, as she went back into the café.

I was on the point of tipping the chips into the bin but decided against it in case Jaimini came back in to try and catch me out. Instead, I tipped in about five of them to start with.

Surely I don't actually have to get myself a pet rat? I thought. Then I suddenly remembered all those pets advertised on the bulletin board. It wouldn't really be any hassle, would it? In fact, it was a great idea, because otherwise I wouldn't get to see Steve again, apart from at his surgery with Hairy – *if* I could get Mrs Stone to agree to let me take Hairy in the first place.

There was something niggling at the back of my mind and I couldn't put my finger on what it was. I paused and frowned in the middle of wiping a plastic bowl, then suddenly realized that the one big flaw in my wonderful scheme was the fact that I hadn't actually got the great affinity with animals that I was claiming to have. I began to wonder whether or not a vet and psychologist who was crazy about animals would be easy to fool, and decided a bit rapidly that they wouldn't. Oh, what the heck! I'd have to cross that bridge when I came to it.

For the next twenty minutes I worked hard, going out of the kitchen with orders and into the kitchen with trays of dirty plates. I know I've got the reputation for always having things go wrong when I'm on duty, but I can honestly say the only tiny little thing that went wrong in that twenty minutes was when I bent forward to put a tray down and someone walked past me at that precise moment. I hadn't realized how far my bottom was sticking out, and the person walking past bashed into it which made me do a sort of crash landing into the table I was serving. I put my hand out to break my fall, and it landed splat on a toasty cheese sandwich which completely squashed the sandwich and left my hand covered in grease. Without thinking I wiped my hand on my school skirt, which won't please Mum too much. Still, all in all, that's fairly minor for me.

I replaced the sandwich and, as soon as I had a second, nipped over to the bulletin board and scoured it for rats for sale. Bingo! There were two for sale – both in the same advert. The telephone number was local, too. Even better! I repeated it to myself all the way back to the kitchen, then wrote it down and stuffed it in my school bag before deciding it was safe to chuck the rest of the chips into the bin. Then I went back into the café.

Jaimini and the others were just going. Leah offered me another fruit pastille and I took it. Just for good measure, as I said bye to them, I told Jaimini how lovely the chips were. Then I turned to Steve and Donna, who looked as though they were about to go, too.

"So, when's it to be, Lucy?" asked Donna.

I didn't need to ask what she meant. "Whenever you want," I replied lightly, thinking happily how useful it was that my passport to Steve was so keen to see me again.

"Well, I can't manage tomorrow evening, but the following one would be fine," Donna replied eagerly. "What about you, Steve? Are you free on Friday evening?"

"Yep, guess so," replied Steve. It sounded really good the way he said that, and I decided then and there to use that phrase myself a few times. "Is that OK with you, Luce?"

"Yep…" I only just managed to stop myself saying it immediately, which would have sounded stupid. "Yeah, that's fine."

So we settled on six o'clock and when I'd given them directions to my place they went, leaving me with the slightly uneasy feeling that I'd need to get moving if I was to have a rat safely installed, with a cage and whatever else you needed, all in two days. I'd also have to borrow the hairy hound for the occasion, but that shouldn't pose too much of a problem.

I decided to phone the rat advert immediately,

which meant getting a ten-pence piece from my school bag and checking that neither Jan nor Becky was watching. Becky is the other person who works at the same time as we do. Either Becky or Mark is always on duty with us. They're both really nice, but Mark is closer in age to us and more easy-going than Becky. She's a very down-to-earth sort of person in her early twenties. She disapproves of laziness and I know it was only a phone call, but I didn't want to draw attention to myself while I was enquiring about rats!

After only two rings the phone was picked up.

"Hello, is that the place where there's a rat for sale?" I asked.

"Yes, it is," came the answer. It was a woman, and she sounded as though she was fed up with answering the phone.

"Is it still for sale?" I asked, feeling anxious in case I was too late.

"Yes, it is, only 'it' is a 'they'," came the rather confusing reply.

"It's a they?" I repeated slowly, probably sounding really thick.

"I'm not selling them separately. They stay together because they're brothers."

My brain was racing away. Would I be able to explain the added presence of Zinc, Zonc's brother, who was so boring I'd not even bothered to mention him before?

"Er … can I come and have a look at them?" I asked, thinking that maybe she'd change her mind when I actually turned up.

She told me where she lived, which was very handy because it was only about two streets away from my house, so I arranged to go there as soon as I'd finished at the café.

At six-twenty, I was standing in Mrs Gadsby's kitchen, peering in at these two identical-looking rats in a cage, and trying to think of intelligent things to say about them. All my ideas about buying only one of them had been instantly squashed because of Mrs Gadsby's opening comment. She didn't sound unkind or anything, just firm.

"You're the fifth person to come and look at them, but no one's taken them because everyone only wants one, and as I said to you on the phone, I'm not letting them go separately because they're brothers and they'd miss each other."

"That's OK, I'll take them both," I said impulsively, because after all, what difference did it make whether I had one or two? The only problem was what to actually take them home in.

"Um, I haven't got anything to take them in…" I began hesitantly, feeling stupid for not having thought about that before.

"Well, you can take the cage they're in if you

want. I was going to sell it eventually because I'm not planning on having any more rats now Charlie's gone."

"Charlie?" I asked.

"My youngest son. They've all kept rats. All three of my sons. We've had so many rats in and out of this house over the years that I nearly renamed the place Rat Palace."

She smiled at me and I decided that I really liked her.

"The only trouble is I've only got six pounds on me," I told her.

"You may as well take it, love," she said, "and here's a bit of hay and food chucked in. How's that, hm?"

"That's brilliant!" I answered her.

"Here you are, have a piece of coconut cake, fresh out of the oven," she went on.

"Um, I'm afraid I'm allergic to coconut, actually," I said, thinking how clever I was getting at inventing excuses for not eating.

"Oh, not to worry, bet you're not allergic to chocolate, are you?" she grinned as she opened a tin to reveal KitKats and Bourbon biscuits. My mouth watered but I hesitated for a second. When I looked up from the tin, my eyes met Mrs Gadsby's eyes. They were regarding me knowingly. I blushed and quickly took a KitKat. The next moment she was back to normal, thank goodness, but the look in her eyes was to stay with me for quite a while, though I didn't know it then.

"Thanks," I said, stuffing the KitKat into my pocket. "I'd better be going," I added, before she started insisting that I ate the KitKat in front of her.

"Take care," she said quietly, as I was going.

I just smiled because I wasn't sure whether she meant of myself or of her rats.

All the way home I planned what to say to Mum about the rats. Everything I thought of seemed so unsuitable, or even completely ridiculous, that in the end I decided there was only one thing I could do and that was to smuggle them in without saying anything. I would keep them in the garden shed because it's a big shed and it's absolutely full of stuff. Mum loves gardening, when she's not cooking or writing poetry, but because she's quite disorganized, everything is all heaped up in the shed, any-old-how. I knew Mum, and she kept the stuff she needed regularly for gardening at the front of the shed. So it would be perfectly safe to keep Zinc and Zonc at the back, behind the deckchairs, for example. Tim and Leo might be a problem, though. It was impossible to keep anything secret from Tim and Leo in our house. I might have to bribe them to keep quiet.

When I got home, I nipped round the side and popped my head furtively round the corner, to check Mum wasn't at the kitchen window or anything. She wasn't, so I quickly slipped into the shed and dumped the cage on the floor at the back, making sure it wasn't in view from the door, then I let myself into the house.

"Hi, Mum," I called.

"Hi, love. Good day?"

"Yeah, fine. Where's Terry?" I always go to talk to Terry if he's home, as soon as I get in, because he's the most brilliant stepfather in the world. He's a very cuddly, kind person, totally unfit and overweight, hasn't got much patience with people he doesn't like, but he's been lovely to me from the very first moment he ever set eyes on me which was ten years ago. I'm far closer to him than to my real dad.

"He's gone, love," Mum replied, gently.

"Gone? Where?"

"To Wales. Remember? He did hang on and wait for you for a little while but in the end he had to go."

"Oh, no!" I said, slowly and quietly, while sinking heavily into the nearest chair. "I'd completely forgotten he was going today..." And I had. Terry was going to Wales on business for a few days and I'd not even said goodbye. For a moment I wanted to kick myself. After all, if I

56

hadn't wasted time getting the rats, I wouldn't have missed Terry, would I?

"Can I phone him on his mobile?" I asked Mum.

"Go on, then. What made you late, by the way?"

"I dropped in on Fen to give her something," I answered vaguely. I knew Mum, and as long as I kept my tone very vague she wouldn't take any notice of me. If I'd invented a more detailed, precise reason for being late, she might have smelt a rat! Literally!

"Where've you been?" Tim asked, shooting through the kitchen door on his spindly legs and rushing to the surface near the cooker to see what titbits Mum had left lying around.

"None of your business," I answered, but I needn't have bothered because he wasn't listening.

"What time's tea? I'm starving."

"Oh, no set time. You know what it's like when Dad's not here. It's more a question of fending for yourself."

"Oh, Luce, make me something, will you?" Tim begged, turning pleading eyes on me. Leo came in at that point and joined in the assault.

I didn't mind. I was actually feeling quite relieved that, for the next few days at least, my eating habits wouldn't be under the microscope quite so much. At least there was *one* good thing about Terry being away.

"Stick a pizza in the oven," Mum said, flying past me with some flan cases that she was about to grease.

So I did, and then I had a long conversation with Terry. I very nearly told him about the rats, but decided that it would be foolish, because even Terry had his cut-off point, and I reckoned that telling him I'd brought two pet rats into the home without telling Mum might just be pushing my luck a bit.

I managed to get through to bed time without eating anything more than a thin little sliver of pizza and an apple. I was pretty sure Mum hadn't noticed because she was so busy with her catering order, and when she'd finished that, she crashed out in front of the television.

Weighing myself in my room a bit later, I found that I'd lost four more pounds! This made me feel absolutely ecstatic. I tried on lots of my clothes in front of the mirror to see if I looked any better in any of them, and I thought on balance that I probably did.

My homework was a dead loss because I couldn't concentrate due to massive hunger pangs which put me on some sort of high. I felt very restless, so it obviously wasn't true about needing food to give you energy.

I went to bed early because I didn't want to prolong the awful feeling of starving, but I couldn't get to sleep because of the amazing high feeling I had, so in the end I decided that I'd just eat the KitKat that was still in my pocket. Having made the decision to eat it I couldn't get it down fast enough and then I felt *really* hungry – much more hungry than before I'd eaten it. It was so unbearable that I had to go downstairs.

Mum was still asleep in front of the television so I sneaked into the kitchen and opened the fridge. There were so many goodies in there it was hard to know what to choose. In the end, although I would have much preferred a dough-nut, or a piece of flan, I took a stick of celery. But even as I was eating it, my mind was on the next thing I was going to eat, because I'd come to the point where I just couldn't hold out any longer. I'd given in. I knew that nothing could stop me eating now. It was a big relief in a way, because the pressure was off.

So I cut myself a piece of the beautiful cheese and onion flan that Mum had made. There were three flans in the fridge, but Mum often made an extra one of whatever she was making for her clients for us lot, so I wasn't worried about digging in. That piece of flan was absolutely heavenly. I don't think I've ever eaten anything so quickly in my life, and before I knew it I was cutting myself a second slice, then a third and then a fourth. I ate every piece as fast as the last one and all the while my mind was working away: *It doesn't matter because I've hardly eaten a thing today, so I'm allowed this. After all it's just a snack, not a proper meal.*

There was only one piece left and it seemed stupid to leave it so I stuffed it down quickly before I could change my mind. Then when I'd swallowed the last bit of it, I stared at the empty flan case and felt awful. What if Mum *hadn't* made an extra one for us? What if she needed all three for the client? As I was thinking this, I distinctly heard a noise in the other room.

Omigod! Mum was waking up! I grabbed the empty flan dish and put it in the dishwasher, then returned to the food cupboard and stared in there, timing it so that my hand was reaching for a chocolate finger as the door opened.

"I thought you'd gone to bed," Mum said, looking bleary-eyed.

"I just popped down for something to eat," I said.

"Oh, Luce, I'm a terrible mother," said Mum, with a sleepy smile. "Tell you what, to make up for having no proper meal together today, we'll have a Chinese tomorrow, OK?"

"OK," I said, trying to sound enthusiastic while working out how much I would have to deny myself during the following two days, to make up for tonight's binge, and tomorrow night's Chinese.

"Night, Mum."

"Night, love."

That night I didn't do the hands round the waist test. I felt grumpy and depressed because I'd spoilt my diet. My last thought before going to sleep was: *Right, I'll start again tomorrow and I won't ever fall into that trap again. I'll be strong willed. Nothing will break my resolve until I'm as thin as Fen.*

Chapter 4

The next day after school I went to drama club. I was feeling on top form as I went into the hall where the class takes place. I'd managed to get through the day so far without eating anything at all and I'd got that lovely energetic feeling that made me believe I could do whatever I wanted to do. Quite honestly, I wouldn't have been surprised if I'd found I could fly. It was true my stomach was contracting because it was so desperate for food, but I knew it was going to have some Chinese later, so it would just have to manage without until then. I was hoping that Sally would notice how slim I was and change her mind about Annie. I sucked in my cheeks and looked right at her as she began to address us all.

"Right, I told you last week that we're going to start rehearsals for the show, didn't I? So, now I'm going to tell you what we're doing and then we'll do a few mini-auditions to see who's going to take what part."

Brilliant, I thought, sitting up straight and getting ready to concentrate like mad. Even though I wanted to do *Annie* I also wanted a good part in my own class's production. There were twenty people in the class, fourteen girls and six boys, and everybody in the class was pretty good at acting and singing, and most were good dancers, too. So, in other words, there was plenty of competition.

"We're going to have a shot at *Blood Brothers*," Sally went on. As soon as she said this a great wave of excitement went round the class as everyone wondered what parts there were. I knew the story of the play *Blood Brothers*, and I thought I'd like to play the part of Micky's girlfriend. I could remember her in the show when I'd seen it and she was really nice-looking. The main part was Mrs Johnson, but I didn't want to do that particularly. It didn't seem the right sort of part for me, somehow. Mrs Johnson was quite a dowdy sort of person.

"What are the other classes doing?" asked a boy called Keith.

"The eight-to-elevens are doing *Annie*, and the young ones are doing *Rumplestiltskin*," Sally told him.

The moment she said that I stared hard at her

again, but I must have let a sigh escape or something because Sally looked straight back at me.

"What's the matter, Lucy?" she asked, pleasantly enough.

"I ... I was just thinking about *Annie*. I really like that show…"

"I agree it's a great show, but as I said to Megan, it's much more suitable for younger children. We don't want great big teenagers clumping about the stage, do we?" She laughed and everybody joined in – everyone except me, that is. Couldn't she see that I'd lost weight? She made me sick. Sally must have noticed my straight face, though, because she immediately went on to list the cast and asked me to try for the part of Mrs Johnson.

As soon as she said that, several faces looked with great envy in my direction, because everyone knew that was the best part. So why wasn't I excited? All I could think about was being Annie. I had the right sort of hair for it. I even – get this! – had a dog who would follow me about anywhere I went, just like the dog who follows Annie in the show.

I auditioned for Mrs Johnson without much enthusiasm, because I had a plan. At the end of the class I was going to beg Sally to let me audition for Annie. When I told her about Hairy she might be a bit keener, then she'd look at me properly and see that not all thirteen-year-olds were clumpy.

Sally auditioned three other girls for the part of Mrs Johnson and then said that she couldn't make up her mind and she'd decide by the next lesson. After that, she did a few trials for other parts, then taught us all one of the big numbers. I couldn't concentrate properly because my mind was on the end of the lesson so I could ask about Annie.

"Now, listen carefully all of you," Sally was saying. "I'm having to change next week's class to Wednesday. Can all of you manage that?"

We all said we could, then the moment she said we could go, most people went crashing out of the hall, and the others were all chatting. I waited till Sally was free, then went up to her.

"I know you want small children doing *Annie*, Sally, but I was wondering if there's any chance of me joining in with them? I am quite small for my age and I've got the right hair and I've even got a dog who follows me around."

Sally laughed when I said that. "The trouble is, Lucy, that the other girls will all look so tiny next to you, and the part of Miss Hannagan, who's in charge of the orphanage, is going to be taken by a girl who's very spindly-looking, so we can't have a great big Annie amongst that lot, you see…"

She'd said it again. She'd called me "great

big". This time it really annoyed me. I was probably scowling but I didn't care.

"I thought you'd want the part of Mrs Johnson, Lucy. It's the most fantastic part. It would be a wonderful challenge for you."

I grunted and Sally sighed, then started packing her things away. I was on the point of going home, feeling totally miserable and depressed, when this girl called Kirsty asked me if I'd sponsor her for a famine they were doing at her school. I started to say I couldn't really afford it, then I suddenly realized what she'd just said.

"Sponsored famine? You mean, you don't eat for a while?"

"Twenty-four hours. It's tomorrow. Most people have got plenty of sponsors but I've only got three. Mum suggested I asked around here at the club, but I forgot all about it till now."

"What's the famine in aid of?" I asked, trying to show an interest.

"Down's Syndrome children," she replied, "and you don't have to sponsor me for much. Even if you just give me fifty pence if I manage to do the whole twenty-four hours, that'd be all right."

"Actually, I'm very interested in Down's Syndrome children," I lied. "I don't suppose you've got one of those forms, have you? Or even two, because I could give one to my friend. Then

66

I could sponsor you, if you would sponsor me. So we just keep our fifty pence. OK?"

"I haven't got any more forms, but we could photocopy this one if you want."

"If you want something photocopied, there's a copier in the other room. It'll cost you ten pence," Sally called out, helpfully.

"Oh, yes, please," I said quickly, so she ran me off two copies. I'd have to Tipp-Ex out the bits that Kirsty had already filled in for herself.

On the way home I thought about what Sally had said. Every time I passed a window where I could see my reflection, I held my stomach in and looked carefully at the reflection to see if I *was* "great big". I decided I'd learn a couple of *Annie* songs off by heart and turn up with Hairy on Saturday for the eight-to-elevens class. By Saturday I planned to be as skinny as a rake and that would convince Sally that I would be the perfect choice for the role of Annie.

I'd already formulated a fantastic plan now I was armed with my two famine sponsorship forms. What I was going to do was pretend to Jaimini and the others that the twenty-four-hour famine was for the following day, but to Mum I'd say it was the day after that – Saturday. I'd have to do some careful work with the Tipp-Ex in case Mum noticed the date at the top of the form, but this way I could get through two days without touching a morsel. I just had tonight's Chinese takeaway to get through, and if I was careful I could get away with eating very little.

Before going home I bought some more rat food and hay, then had to smuggle them in without anyone noticing. Unfortunately, Tim and Leo were rollerblading on the footpath outside our house and came rolling up to meet me.

"What's that for?" asked Tim.

"None of your business," I told him, knowing full well that it would *have* to be his business, otherwise he'd tell Mum.

"Tell us, or we'll tell Mum," Leo said, confirming what I already knew, that it was a pain having two small brothers.

"It's hay for my rats, OK? But if you breathe a word to Mum I'll make up something that'll get you grounded for weeks. Got that?"

Their eyes had widened with admiration. "Where are they?" Leo asked, in a loud whisper.

"I'll show you if you promise to be discreet about looking at them. It really is important that Mum doesn't find out I've got them."

"Why *have* you got them?" Tim asked, with the same hushed reverence that Leo had used for the great rat introduction.

"Because they're really good pets, but it's not easy getting an adult to see that. Now, get those blades off," I instructed them, rather bossily, but neither of them argued. They were hooked. The idea that we'd got rats on the premises had probably given them more excitement than they'd had for weeks.

"This one's called Zinc and that one's called Zonc," I whispered, as we all peered in.

"Can we hold them?" they asked, at exactly the same moment. The twins often spoke at exactly the same time, as though they had one brain between the two of them.

"OK then. Get them out," I said, casually. The truth was that I didn't think I dared to handle them myself because their tails were so disgusting.

The twins' hands plunged into the cage at the same moment and miraculously each hand came out carrying a rat. I tried not to shudder and concentrated on putting more hay and food in the cage.

"How do you know which is which?" asked Tim.

I hadn't a clue which was which, but I thought I ought to appear to be totally in control because that's what you have to do with the twins. If they spot that you've got even the teeniest weakness, they use it for their own ends. I learnt years ago how to handle the little pests. I just feel sorry for their teachers, especially when they pretend to be each other, and the poor teacher can't tell if they're kidding or not.

"It's obvious which is which," I said calmly. "I expect I can tell because I've had years of practice at telling the difference between you two."

They spent the next few minutes examining the rats for possible marks of difference and could only come up with one. The one I'd apparently called Zonc had some slightly darker hair just near its tail. I made a mental note to remember this important fact in case my adorable brothers decided to give me a spot check on rat identification at any point.

"Here you are, Luce, hold Zonc a sec while I make their hay a bit cosier," said Tim, handing the revolting creature over to me. It was all I could do not to pass out on the spot, especially when it twined its tail round my fingers, then scuttled up my arm and stuck its horrid pointy nose into my neck.

"I think we'd better put them back in their cage now," I said, trying not to cringe, or look too petrified and stiff. "I haven't even said hello to Mum yet, and I don't want her coming in here and finding them, do I?"

Tim was bending down, peering into the food bag, at that moment, and Leo, unexpectedly agreeing with me straight away, plonked Zinc into the cage. He then unpeeled Zonc from my shoulder to put him in the cage, too. What the stupid boy forgot to do was shut the door on

Zinc. We both realized this fatal mistake at the same time, but by then, it was too late. I watched with horror as Zinc scooted across the shed floor and out of the door. Leo was so mesmerized, he very nearly dropped Zonc as well.

"Get Zonc in the cage and shut the door," I hissed at him furiously. "Tim, come and help me catch Zinc. If Mum comes across a rat, she'll go berserk. Honestly Leo, how *could* you be so utterly idiotic?"

I didn't wait for a reply, just belted into the back garden and began searching. After about five minutes, Mum came outside.

"Hello, love. I didn't know you were back… What … what are you doing exactly?"

"Biology homework," I told her quick as a flash. "I've got to examine the soil, you see."

"Examine the soil? What, to see if it's clay soil or something?"

"Yes, and various other things, and things about plants too … and weeds," I added, thinking it sensible to have as many angles on this homework as possible in case I had to explain why it was necessary to be out in the garden for such a long time.

"Are the twins helping you?" asked Mum, the tiniest hint of suspicion creeping into her voice because, let's face it, the twins were not renowned for their eagerness to help with my homework.

"They're seeing who can find the most worms," I said, with a sort of "trust *them*!" look.

Mum smiled and said she'd make me a sandwich because I must be starving. I quickly assured her that a girl from drama had given me a bag of crisps, and she went in, thank goodness.

After twenty minutes, I decided to give up.

"With any luck it will have gone next door," I said, and realized immediately that that was the wrong thing to say.

"But don't you care that you've lost one of your pets when you've only just got them?" Tim asked, his voice getting higher and higher with indignation.

"Oh, yes, I'm heartbroken, of course," I quickly corrected my mistake, but I didn't sound very convincing, even to myself. "I'll come out later, when you two have gone to bed," I added.

"It'll be dark by then," Leo pointed out.

"I'll take a torch."

We all went in, and I went straight upstairs to get away from the food. I was starving by this time and starting to weaken just like I had done the previous day. Then I thought about Sally Ahlers and what she'd said. *Great big*. I'd show her. Maybe I'd go and pay a visit to Hairy. I needed to check he still wanted to follow me everywhere. After all, Hairy was part of my great plan to get the role in *Annie*.

"I'm just going to see Hairy," I told Mum. "I won't be long."

"I've ordered the Chinese. I'm going to go and get it in twenty minutes, so make sure you're back by then," said Mum.

Mrs Stone greeted me a little less fondly than I thought she would, but I soon realized that it was only because she was disappointed that her new-found pet wasn't living up to her expectations.

"I wondered if I could say hello to Hairy," I smiled.

"Kenneth!" she called, in a sing-song, stupid voice that made me want to crack up.

Hairy didn't appear, and Mrs Stone's face immediately took on a teacherish look. "He's not exactly the most obedient dog under the sun, is he?" she said, rather sadly.

Oh, dear. This wasn't working out very well for poor Mrs Stone. I reckoned that if I asked to have him back, she'd probably hand him over without any resistance. Mum wouldn't be too happy, though. No, it would be better all round if I just had visitation rights to Hairy, but didn't actually own him. I did want to be the one to take him to the vet, though, and of course I needed to borrow him for Steve and Donna's visit the following evening.

"Hairy!" I called brightly, and immediately the great lolloping hound came plodding slowly through to the kitchen where we were. He put his paw up on my leg but let it drop almost immediately as though he didn't have the energy to keep it there. Then he rested his head against my leg.

"He's definitely got a thing about you, hasn't he?" remarked Mrs Stone, with the same anxious expression.

"I've no idea why," I said, patting Hairy, but not really feeling any great affection towards him. It's not that I don't like dogs or anything, just that I'm not exactly dog mad, like most of my friends are.

"I was thinking perhaps I ought to take him to the vet," I said, holding my breath, and hoping that Mrs Stone wouldn't tell me that she'd already done that.

"Fine by me," she said, to my great relief. "Just let me know when and I'll have him spruced up and ready."

"I'll make the appointment tomorrow. It'll probably be for Monday."

"Fine by me," she said, again.

"I'd better get back because Mum's going out and she wants me to be at home for the twins," I excused myself. There didn't seem any reason to stay any longer because I'd established that Hairy still remembered me, and the following evening I would simply turn up and ask if I could take him home for a bit.

"Hope you manage it," said Mrs Stone. I didn't know what she was talking about until I found myself being followed by the devoted Hairy. Not a single bribe would make the stupid dog stay with his new owner. He just wagged his tail and followed, one pace behind me. In the end, I had to go back into the kitchen, wait for Mrs Stone to hang on to his collar, then slip out of the door as fast as I could, pulling it closed behind me. As I was walking away I could hear Hairy crying. He really was a crazy dog!

A bit later Mum came back with the Chinese takeaway and we set the little tin foil trays out all over the kitchen table. It smelt absolutely wonderful and my mouth was really watering. The twins were hopping about excitedly, each trying to get a bit of everything on to his plate before the other one did. Mum was slowly serving herself, and I was standing there wondering what on earth to do.

"Come on, Luce, dive in," Mum smiled.

"I feel terrible when you've gone to all this trouble, Mum, but the thing is, I'm not all that hungry…"

She stopped what she was doing with her spoon above her plate. "Not hungry? Why?" she asked, simply.

"It may be because Sally brought in a big cake to drama. It was her birthday, you see, so we all had huge slices, and that was on top of the crisps I got from Joanna West."

"Never mind," said Mum, quite brightly. "Just have a little bit, and maybe you'll feel like some more later."

Her eyes met mine and something in them reminded me of that look in Mrs Gadsby's eyes. She didn't see through me, did she? They hadn't both seen through me, had they? No, of course not. I was worrying about nothing. I put a tiny bit on my plate and began to eat it very slowly. It tasted like the most wonderful food in the world. I took a second mouthful and thought it tasted even better. The third and fourth mouthfuls followed much more quickly, the fifth and sixth I devoured so fast anyone'd think I hadn't eaten for a month, and then I'd finished all that was on my plate. I looked at the row of half-full trays, then I looked at Mum. She was surveying me with her head on one side and that same knowing expression in her eyes.

"Well, for someone who wasn't hungry, that went down amazingly quickly," she commented. I was torn then, because I'd made a big mistake. I'd more or less demonstrated that although I'd *said* I wasn't hungry, really I was starving. So either I gave in and admitted my lie, *or* I quickly thought of some reason for why I'd been in such a hurry. I was just debating this problem in my head when I was stopped in my mental tracks by the most appalling sight.

Up on the curtain pole sat Zinc, washing himself calmly. I forced myself to drag my eyes away from him, so that Mum's attention wouldn't be alerted, but unfortunately Tim had caught my expression of horror and had noticed the rat. His eyes were big and round, and at any moment he would give the game away, so I kicked him hard under the table which made him look at me long enough for me to warn him with my eyes to shut up.

I risked another glance at the curtain pole and got a second horrible shock because Zinc had disappeared. By this time I really *didn't* feel hungry. Every fibre in my body was taken up with the problem of catching an escaped rat and removing it from the room without Mum noticing. Just then, something caught the corner of my eye. Zinc was down by the bin. And Mum was getting up with her plate!

"It's OK, Mum, I'll do that. You sit still. You should relax more, you know," I gabbled. "Shouldn't she?" I appealed to the twins. Leo, who hadn't yet noticed Zinc, looked at me as though I'd got a screw loose, but Tim did a sort of gulp and said "Yes, Mum, you should relax more. Luce is quite right."

This little speech, being so totally out of

character for Tim, made Leo positively gawp at his twin and ask, in true Leo fashion, "What are you on about?"

Mum's eyes narrowed but she agreed to stay seated while I took her plate and loaded it into the dishwasher. The pedal bin was about a metre from the dishwasher and I was dreading Zinc skidding across the kitchen floor in an attempt to get away from my feet. But he didn't move. He carried on his washing activities as though he hadn't a care in the world, which he probably hadn't. Then the phone rang.

Mum pushed her chair back to get up, but again I leapt over to her and told her not to move because I would answer the phone. Then I realized the phone wasn't anywhere in the kitchen, because it's one of those portable ones. I didn't dare leave the kitchen, though, so it was probably better on balance if Mum *did* answer the phone because that at least would get her out of the kitchen.

"Oh, OK, *you* get the phone, Mum, and us three will get this whole kitchen cleared and tidied away before you get back." I gave her a big smile and guided her to the door. She allowed herself to be banished from the room, but it was obvious she thought something was going on. I just had to pray that she put all the secretive stuff down to me wanting to give her a nice surprise.

The moment she'd left the room I instructed

Tim to pick up Zinc, and go and put him back in his cage. Tim approached Zinc as though approaching a poisonous snake, but luckily managed to grab him without any trouble. The only little moment of tension came when Leo, who still didn't know what was going on, suddenly clicked on and cried out, "Oh, it's the rat! You've found it, haven't you?"

"Shut up, Leo!" I screeched, jerking my head at the door Mum had gone through, then I pushed Tim out of the back door and shut it as Mum reappeared through the other door. I must have been looking guilty as anything.

"It's someone called Donna, for you," said Mum.

My heart missed a beat as my brain played through the imaginary dialogue that might have just passed between Mum and Donna.

"Hello, is that Lucy's mother?"

"Y … yes?"

"I'm terribly sorry I don't actually know your surname, but I met Lucy in the café yesterday and she was talking about her great affinity with animals. Anyway, to cut a long story short I'm supposed to be coming to see her rat tomorrow night, but I can't make it, so could I possibly have a word with her, please?"

Mum handed the phone to me without show-ing any sign that she'd just had a mad woman raving about rats on the line, so I decided that Donna couldn't have spilt the beans after all.

"Hello, Donna."

"Hello, Lucy. Look, I'm really sorry, something's come up and I'm not going to be able to make tomorrow evening or the next few evenings, so, I know it's terribly short notice, but is there any chance that I could come along tonight? I've cancelled what I was going to be doing and Steve says he can come, too."

My brain was in a flat spin. I couldn't possibly have Donna and Steve at the house with Mum there. By the following evening I would have thought of a way to get Mum out of the place for a little while, but there was no way I could do anything now. I glanced at Mum and saw that although she was pretending not to listen, she was obviously eaten up with curiosity about who this Donna could be. I casually strolled out of the kitchen and it was then that I had a great idea.

"Actually, it's not all that convenient this evening because I've got to help Mum, you see. I could bring them to the café at about four o'clock tomorrow, though, if you wanted?" I offered enthusiastically, knowing as I said it that the café was the worst possible place to have suggested for showing someone your rat.

"Them? I thought you just had the one rat," Donna immediately pointed out.

What a stupid mistake to make! "Sorry, I meant 'it'. It's just that I'm so used to saying 'them' about my twin brothers. I sometimes feel as thought I've got two of everything," I went on glibly.

She laughed and said she wasn't sure that the café was the ideal place to take a rat, but we agreed to meet in the café and then go on to somewhere like the rec, which was within walking distance.

"Who's Donna?" Mum asked, when I went back into the kitchen a moment later.

"She's just someone I met in the café," I told Mum. "She's really nice and she's studying applied psychology and she's interested in how I can imitate people so easily when I'm acting. It's part of her course, you see."

Mum nodded and opened the dishwasher, before turning very slowly round to face me.

"Did you eat the third cheese and onion flan, Luce?" she asked softly.

"No!"

The word was out before I'd even had time to think. Now it was out I had to stick with it. "Course not," I added indignantly. "I'd better start my homework," I quickly went on, trying to look as ordinary and unruffled as possible.

As I left the room I heard Mum say, "Look, you two, if I find out that you're lying to me, and you *did* eat that flan, I'll be furious and ground you for a whole month."

I didn't listen to any more. It was all getting so complicated.

Never mind, it was worth it, I thought a few minutes later when I stood on the scales and saw that my weight was back down again after the previous night's binge. Thank goodness for Zinc! If he hadn't appeared at that moment I would have scoffed down the whole of the rest of the Chinese takeaway without it even touching the sides!

Chapter 5

After school the next day, Friday, I walked down to the café with Jaimini. It was Andy's turn to work, and the other three had gone on ahead of Jaimes and me. It had been a funny day because something had changed. I had shown the famine sponsorship form to Jaimes and the others and they'd all filled in their names quite happily and offered fifty pence if I completed the twenty-four hours without any food. Jaimini had hesitated and asked me if I was sure it was a good idea, but I think I convinced her that it was no big deal and in the end she promised seventy-five pence, and a few other people in my tutor group had sponsored me too, including my teacher.

I'd therefore got the perfect excuse not to eat. The reason it was a funny day was because I really didn't feel like eating anyway. In fact, it was absolutely no effort at all not to eat. My body seemed to have adjusted to it. As I'd walked around school I'd felt as though I was floating just above the floor, and in the lessons I'd been able to concentrate much better. Two teachers had even commented on how impressed they were with me.

Jaimini and I were discussing Zonc and Zinc for about the fiftieth time that day. You see, the previous evening, after the scare in our kitchen, I'd reached a decision. I'd decided that I had to get rid of these rats and the sooner the better. So I had tried to persuade all my friends how wonderful it would be to have two pet rats.

Jaimes had said, "I would no more be allowed to keep a couple of rats in the house, than I'd be allowed to keep a couple of gorillas, Luce!"

Fen had been tempted, but felt it wouldn't be fair to her newly acquired rabbit if she had to split her affections. Tash had said she thought her Mum was finding their dog Boo quite enough of a handful. Leah had said that they didn't have enough room in the garden for any more than her guinea pigs, and Andy hadn't said anything.

Now, I've told you about Andy. She's a very daring person, but she also has very definite views on things, and I knew very well that as far as the question of keeping rats was concerned, it all depended on whether Andy really wanted rats. If she *did*, she would somehow overcome any hurdles that got in her way to make sure she could have them. *If* she did!

When I'd asked her a second time, she'd said, "Mum'd kill me."

"So don't tell her," I'd suggested.

"Dad'd kill me."

The others had practically winced when she'd said that because, like I said, they're all afraid of Andy's dad.

"So don't tell *him*," I'd suggested, as calmly as I could.

She'd stayed silent and thoughtful for at least two minutes, then she'd just said "OK" as though she was merely agreeing to lend me a book or something.

I'd got the rats at school because I was taking them straight to the café afterwards, then Andy was going to take them home with her at the end of her duty.

We'd had a great time keeping them away from the teachers. At break time we'd taken them down to the netball courts. Andy was the only one of us who dared to handle them. It was obvious she was growing attached to them, and it was while she was letting Zonc run all over her body, up her arm, across her shoulders and down the other arm, that Jaimes pointed out something that was to prove invaluable for my "affinity with animals" bit!

Jaimes, being the observant, intelligent type, had pointed out that Zinc had about twice as much energy as Zonc. Zonc just wanted to stay with you all the time, like a good, sociable little rat, but Zinc tried to run away at every available opportunity. It seemed to me that I could use this fact to further my cause. And I was trying to persuade Jaimes to help me with my brilliant plan to fool Donna and Steve and make them think I really *did* have an extraordinary affinity with animals as we walked down to the café. Donna and Steve were going to meet me there.

"Go on, Jaimes, it'll be ever so easy. You'll see."

"But it's deliberately deceiving them," Jaimes pointed out, with an anxious look on her face that reminded me of one of Leah's worried looks.

"But it's not a big deceive."

"Deception. It's not a big deception."

"There you are. I knew you'd agree in the end."

"But I don't agree!"

"You just said, 'It's not a big deception.'"

"I wasn't saying that. I was just correcting you."

"Oh… Well, anyway… Oh, go *on*, Jaimes. Be a gem," I pleaded.

"If I *do*," she said, very slowly, "will you promise not to do any other deceitful animal stuff?"

"I do solemnly swear never (after this) to do

any other deceitful animal stuff," I said, in my most reverent tones.

There was a long pause while Jaimes considered this, then, blow me if she didn't say she couldn't do it anyway!

"Why *ever* not?" I asked, getting exasperated, because we were almost at the café and I was relying on Jaimes to make my whole plan work.

"Because I don't like handling the rats, so I'd mess it up, and I'm not comfortable with lying."

"But you wouldn't be lying…"

"Look, why don't you just ask Andy?" said Jaimini, sounding cross, and turning away from me.

"OK, I *will*," I told her rather snappily, and we didn't speak for the rest of the walk to the café.

Once inside, we saw that Fen, Tash and Leah had got a table for three, and there wasn't any room for us two, so we had to sit on our own. I really didn't want to sit with Jaimes as she was being so unhelpful to her best friend, so I dumped the rats' cage down in the corner, then went off to the kitchen to find Andy.

Andy was peeling potatoes. She glanced up and smiled when she saw me. I'd passed Jan on my way into the kitchen and she'd said hello and not seemed to mind that I was heading for the kitchen even though I wasn't on duty. Kevin was in his usual good spirits, singing something I didn't recognize which had very few words and a lot of da's in it. He pretended not to have seen me and without changing the song he was singing, he sang the words, "Now, trouble's on its way, I can sense it in the air, Is it here to stay, with its crazy mop of hair?"

"Ha ha, very funny," I responded, then I launched straight in with my plan to Andy.

She listened with a frown of concentration on her face and I got the distinct feeling that she was pretty impressed.

"So will you help me?" I asked her finally.

"No way," she answered abruptly, without even stopping peeling potatoes for a single second.

"Why not?" I asked, feeling really narked.

"Because Steve and Donna would have to be blind and stupid not to see through that plan!" she replied, rather cruelly I thought. I felt my hackles rising. Two out of five friends were prepared to let me completely lose face in front of someone who they knew very well meant a great deal to me. I thought about asking the others but I knew I wouldn't be able to bear it if they all said no, so I stuck my chin in the air and told Andy I didn't need her help anyway, because I could probably manage much better without her.

"Good, I'm glad to hear it," she answered coolly, then she really got me by saying, "Do you still need my help to take the rats home with me afterwards, or have you decided you can manage better without me for that as well?"

"I'll keep the rats," I said aggressively, because I couldn't bear to give her the satisfaction of thinking I needed her in any way, shape or form, *ever*!

When I went back into the café, Jaimini was sitting with the others and it was obvious from their sudden silence when I appeared that Jaimini had told them we'd fallen out. Well, I didn't care. Stuff them! I'd show them. They'd soon change their tune when they heard that I had managed to trick Steve and Donna, and no harm had been done. It made me sick the way that Jaimini was so pious about everything and wouldn't do a single thing that was remotely risky, and Andy was so scathing, always thinking her plans were the best ones and no one else had even *heard* of inventing decent plans.

"Come and sit down, Luce," said Tash. Even *she* irritated me. Why did she always have to be so kind and nice all the time? Why couldn't she break the odd rule now and again, or call some-one something nasty or something?

"I'm all right over here," I said, sitting at a table for two as far away from them as possible.

"Can I get you something, Luce?" asked Jan gently, appearing at my side.

"A Coke, please," I said, trying not to sound too

rude, even though I felt like being rude to everyone at that moment – well, everyone except Steve and Donna, that is.

As soon as I'd said it I remembered my famine, and the last thing I wanted was one of my so-called "friends" pointing out that I shouldn't be drinking Coke because of the *rules*!

"Actually, I'll have a cup of tea with no milk," I said. "I'm doing this famine in aid of children with Down's Syndrome," I explained briefly.

"How much longer have you got to go?" asked Jan, in that same sympathetic tone.

"The rest of the day."

"Oh, poor you. Is it really tough?" she asked, sounding maddeningly sympathetic!

I was about to tell her I was doing perfectly well, thank you very much, when something across the café caught my eye, and I realized with horror that there was a little toddler bending down, fiddling with the door to my rats' cage!

I shot across the café like greased lightning and was only just in time to prevent the unthinkable from happening. Jan followed me at a slightly slower pace to see what on earth was going on and as she arrived, the toddler burst into tears because he must have thought he had been doing something naughty. His mother then came and picked him up and wanted to know what was in the cage. I looked from Jan to the smiling, interested mother and decided that a hamster would go down better than two rats, so that's what I told her.

"Oh, how sweet! Can Sam hold it? He loves little furry things, don't you, Sam?"

"Well, he'd better not," I said, a bit doubtfully. "The thing is, it's asleep during the day, you see, and I don't want to disturb it."

"It's not a good idea having little animals like that in the café," Jan said firmly, giving me a meaningful look, that said, "*What on earth are you thinking about, bringing a hamster into a place serving food, Luce? If this customer wasn't here, I'd be going spare with you!*"

As soon as Sam and his mother had gone back to their table, Jan told me to put the cage at the end of the passage leading to the loos, and make sure the cage door was facing the wall. I did as I was told and thought that even Jan was being unreasonable now. As I went back to my place I saw that it had been taken by two young women and there was nowhere else for me to sit.

"Come and sit with us, Luce," Tash said, for the second time. *She must be going for a Hearts of Gold award or something*, I thought crossly. It made me even crosser that I couldn't turn down this great offer because there was nowhere else to sit. So I sat there, but didn't make any attempt at conversation. I sipped my tea which Jan had brought, and noticed with great satisfaction that Jaimini was looking extremely uncomfortable and worried. *Good*, I thought. *Serves you right!*

After a minute or two of listening to the others prattling on about something that had happened in Leah's orchestra practice that was about as interesting as last week's weather forecast, I started to stare round the café, and that was when I noticed Steve and Donna coming in.

"Hi!" I greeted them happily. It was wonderful to see them after having to suffer sitting in silence, while everyone was chatting and laughing around me – well, everyone except Jaimini.

As luck would have it, a table for three suddenly became free so I grabbed it, and Donna and Steve came smiling over to me. They ordered tea for two and started chatting straight away about me and my rat, which was exactly what I felt like chatting about.

"Have you got him?" asked Donna, looking round.

"Yes, he's in the passage. Jan didn't want him in the café," I grinned.

"Understandable," Steve smiled. It was a very special sort of smile, I thought, and decided that my weight loss was probably noticeable already because Steve was leaning forwards and definitely showing more interest in me than in Donna.

We sipped our tea, and I explained to them that

I'd agreed to let a neighbour of ours look after Hairy for a little while as she was so besotted with him, then I went on to tell them what had happened when I'd been to visit the devoted dog the previous evening. They stared at me open-mouthed and laughed when I got to the bit about Mrs Stone calling Hairy, Kenneth. *If they're impressed by that, wait till they see what I can do to make a rat calm down!* I thought, hugging to me the lovely feeling of being able to do something really well. A shadow crossed my mind when I allowed myself to remember for a second that I couldn't *really* do what I was about to pretend to do, but I pushed the shadow away. It was only a detail, anyway.

My plan was to sit in front of the cage with Steve and Donna behind it. (I'd tell them that for my affinity to be at its best, I needed to be in touch with the rat's home, and the rat mustn't be distracted by the presence of anyone else, so that was why it was better for them to be at the other side of the cage.) I was then going to get Zinc out and show them what a fidgety, crazy rat he was, then I was going to put him back in the cage, shut the door and talk to him in my most calming tones, after which I would take Zonc out and they would see a big difference, without realizing that this was another rat entirely!

"So, where should we go for this demonstration, then, Lucy?" asked Steve.

"And what exactly are you going to demonstrate?" asked Donna.

"Well, I think the rec would be best, like we said. It's not too far. What I'm going to do is try to calm my rat down. I do it every day because Zonc's a really wild rat. He rushes about in a demented sort of way and I'm sure he's not very happy. But I somehow feel as though he's more serene when I've talked to him."

"What? You simply talk to him?" asked Donna, wide-eyed.

"In a certain tone," I told her.

"Perhaps she's hypnotizing the rat," Donna said, turning her big eyes on Steve. I wished she wouldn't do that. She looked far too pretty, and that made me feel ugly.

"Let's have a cake or something. I'm starving," Donna went on brightly.

I was aware that the others were taking in most of our conversation. They were trying not to show that they were listening, but it was obvious they were.

"I can't eat anything today. I'm on a famine," I told her, feeling pleased that this was yet another individual thing about me.

"A famine? What do you mean?"

"People have sponsored me not to eat for twenty-four hours and the money goes to the Down's Syndrome Association. I'm the only one who's doing it at my school," I couldn't resist adding.

"You really are full of surprises," Steve said warmly, so I gave him my most modest smile. I just knew I was creating a big impression and the feeling it was giving me was absolutely wonderful.

"Well, we won't bother with cakes, then," Donna said. "It would be positively cruel to sit here munching away when you're not allowed a crumb, poor thing!"

"I don't mind, honestly," I said magnanimously. And it was true. I didn't mind. In fact, I *wanted* them to eat, because it would make me feel even better that I wasn't.

"Why don't we see Zonc right here and now?" Steve suddenly suggested. "There's no need to go all the way to the rec. After all, he's out in the passage. No one will see that we've got a rat, and if someone comes through to the loo, we'll quickly pop him back in the cage." He was looking round brightly, and I was about to launch into my explanation about how they mustn't be in Zonc's view so it would be best if they stood *behind* the cage and let *me* be the one to get Zonc out, when Donna went striding off towards the corridor.

"It's OK, Donna, I'll…" I began, frantically rushing after her, but she was already out in the passage. By the time I'd got to the cage, she had opened the door and was crouched down, reaching in.

Omigod! This was it. The game was up!

But, miracle of miracles, it wasn't! Donna was standing up straight again with Zonc in her hands. She hadn't even looked inside the cage! Even more incredibly, though, she hadn't noticed that there were actually two rats in there. I offered a quick prayer of thanks to whoever might be listening and then froze with horror because Donna had left the door open, and Zinc had rushed out!

Both Donna and Steve turned appalled expressions on Zinc as he scuttled off, heading straight for the café. My heart was hammering against my ribs as I made a lunge for the hellraising rat, but all I succeeded in doing was banging into the door because some poor unsuspecting customer was coming through to the loo. Zinc saw his chance and scrambled into the café with me just behind him. I was fervently wishing I could click my fingers and make everybody fall asleep until I'd got him safely back into his cage.

Mark was on duty with Jan and Andy. Whoever would have guessed that a tall, thickset, athletic seventeen-year-old guy could possibly be afraid of rats? But he was, and unfortunately he was the first to spot Zinc. His eyes came out on organ stops and he bolted to the other end of the café, looking a bit green around the gills.

One or two customers had followed the direction of Mark's panicky gaze and it only took about five seconds before the whole place was in a screaming, chaotic frenzy. Four people, including Leah and Tash, were standing on chairs, hugging themselves and shivering. Fen and Jaimini were hugging each other. Andy was standing there, big-eyed but calm – as usual.

The toddler was crying energetically while his mother was trying to grab him, his buggy and her shopping bags, and get out of the place as quickly as possible. A few other people were following suit. Jan, who had stood there, eyes darting round the room in complete bafflement at first, had now spotted the rat and was looking distraught. Her eyes met mine.

"What do you know about this?" she asked me, in a dangerously low voice.

"Sorry," I said, but it was as though it wasn't really happening. It felt as though I was in a sort of dream. Steve appeared from the corridor with the nearly weeping Donna. He raised his hands and spoke in a loud but calm voice.

"I'm a vet. It's a perfectly harmless pet rat. Try to keep still and quiet, and I'll catch him and return him to his cage."

There was an immediate hush, then people started talking in trembling, giggling whispers. It was a sort of nervous hysteria. Steve and Donna were closing in on Zinc. I couldn't decide whether to help them or not. I decided I wouldn't. I'd heard about cornered rats, and I didn't want Zinc going for my throat. Steve took his jumper off and chucked it on top of Zinc, then, between them, he and Donna managed to pounce on the jumper without crushing Zinc. Steve retrieved the rat from under the jumper and carried him back to the passage and his cage. I assumed that Donna must have put Zonc back in the cage and shut the door before the big chase started. Nobody moved a muscle until Steve returned to the café.

"There, safe and secure in the cage!" He smiled round at everybody, and then slowly things went back to normal. Jan started going round from table to table trying to reassure everybody that this was only a tame rat, which had been brought into the café when it shouldn't have been. She apologized for all the inconvenience and worry, and offered everybody a free drink. She was making a big point of never looking in my direction. Jaimini and the others were starting to go. Not one of them even glanced at me.

I should have been feeling lonely, but I didn't. I felt cross. It was all so unfair. I knew I was going to get all the blame, and yet it was Donna who had let the wretched rat out in the first place. She'd had no right to go opening the door and getting Zonc out without waiting for me.

"I hope you're pleased with the outcome of all that," Steve said, without smiling at me at all.

"It wasn't my fault," I immediately defended myself.

"You might not have been the one to open the cage, but you deliberately led us to believe there was only one rat in there. I presume you were going to try and impress us by pretending the calm rat and the restless rat were one and the same, and that it only grew calm with your wonderful soothing abilities, weren't you?"

I didn't answer. He obviously hated me, so there was no point in trying to change that now. I stared at him with my hardest expression.

"Poor Donna feels absolutely terrible," he went on.

I glanced over to where Donna was talking to Jan. She had one hand over her face and her shoulders were shaking. It was obvious she was either crying or nearly crying. Sure enough, the next moment Jan led her off to the kitchen with an arm round her shoulder. So I was right. *I* would be the one to get all the blame. Steve walked away from me as though he couldn't even bear to be anywhere near me. I looked over to where Andy had been standing. She wasn't there.

She was working at a frenetic pace, clearing tables and serving drinks as though her life depended on it.

Turning abruptly, I marched into the passage, picked up the cage and carried it rather awkwardly back into the café, then out of the front door. I could feel several pairs of eyes boring into my back, and I wanted to turn round and say, "Want a photo, or something?" But I managed to keep my mouth shut. All the way home I had conversations in my head, between me and Steve, then me and Donna, then me and Jaimini, then me and Jan. In every conversation, *I* came out on top.

I felt more and more powerful all the way home, so that by the time I actually got there, I knew I could handle anything. It must have been that feeling that made me go marching in through the back door still holding the cage. There I confronted Mum calmly.

"Whatever's in there, Luce?"

"Two rats, Mum."

"Two rats! Omigod! Get them out of here this minute!"

"I've brought them home to live here, because I like pet rats. I'll put them in the shed."

"Luce, have you gone mad or something?"

I didn't think I'd gone mad, but that strange dreamlike feeling I'd had was still with me.

Chapter 6

When I returned from the shed, Mum was looking very tight-lipped. *Very* tight-lipped, but also something else. She made me sit down.

"What's going on, Luce?"

"What do you mean?"

"You've changed. Something's happened. What is it?"

"Nothing's changed, except that I've got two pet rats now. They're called Zonc and Zinc, by the way. Do you want to see them?"

"You don't sound like yourself, Luce. Come on, love. What's going on in your life? Please tell me what it is."

"It's nothing. I don't know what you're on about."

Mum didn't say anything, but she picked up the phone and dialled a number, then handed me the phone, saying, "For goodness' sake, talk to Terry. Take the phone upstairs if you want. Just talk to him."

I was desperate to talk to Terry, I suddenly realized. More than anything I wished that he was at home and I could snuggle on the settee with him and he would make me feel like his little girl, just like he always had done. I listened bleakly to the endless ringing tone and finally shoved the aerial in, pressed the "talk" button and flopped back on to my bed. All my new-found energy had disappeared. I just wanted to sleep but I couldn't.

Mum tapped on the door a few minutes later and came in when I didn't answer.

"Did you talk to Terry?"

"No reply."

"Well, there will be, a bit later... Why don't you come down and have some lovely Welsh Rarebit? It's all ready."

"No, thanks."

"Are you ill or something, Luce? You must tell me if you're not well."

"Maybe I'm ill. I don't know."

Actually, it would be a good idea to be ill. It would give me another day off food.

"Yeah, I think I've got some sort of bug. I haven't got any energy."

"Have you got stomach ache?"

"No."

"Is your stomach upset?"

"No."

Stupid answer. I should have said yes. I didn't seem to be able to think straight for some reason or other.

"Well, then I *do* think you should have *something* to eat, even it's just a tiny bit."

"It'll make me sick if I have anything to eat."

"I'll make you a drink, then."

She disappeared before I could argue and came back up a minute or two later with some Horlicks. I wished she would go away but she didn't. She sat on my bed, looking round my room for clues, and trying to get me to talk. Her eyes fell on my scales and she seemed about to say something, then changed her mind.

"Have you fallen out with Jaimini?" she asked, finally.

"Sort of," I replied, and that seemed to satisfy her.

"Do you want to talk about it?"

"No."

"Well, look, love, Terry'll probably phone at about ten, but in the meantime if you want to phone him, you can."

I stayed in my room all evening and at about eight-thirty I went to bed without saying "night" to anyone. I put my hands round my waist and my thumbs were only about two inches apart. I looked down at my legs and they didn't look like mine. It was amazing how effective this dieting was. I couldn't understand why everyone didn't do it. I thought about Ellie Cooper and Susanne Hamton, and wondered briefly how they could live with themselves, looking like that. In fact, I wondered how *I'd* managed to live with myself until that point.

There was something unpleasant drifting across my mind as I began to fall asleep, something to do with Jaimini and the others, but it wasn't important. Nothing was important except being thin enough to do *Annie*. I made a resolution to go to Sally Ahlers' house the next day because I couldn't wait till next Wednesday.

The following morning, I woke up very early and felt light as a feather and quite excited that my big *Annie* day had arrived. I jumped out of bed, but had to grab hold of the windowsill because my balance wasn't all that good. I went straight to the loo, then came back and got on the scales with nothing on. Seven-stone-five. Good. But I wanted it in the sixes. I knew Andy weighed something in the sixes.

"Morning, love. Feeling better?" was Mum's greeting.

I ignored that.

"Did Terry phone?"

"Yes, he did … and…"

"When's he coming home?"

"Monday evening." Mum was beaming at me as though I'd be pleased with this news.

"Not till Monday evening? I thought he might be back today."

"Only three more days."

The twins appeared on their rollerblades then, and skated like loonies round the kitchen table for a while, then stopped abruptly at exactly the same moment, and Tim said, "Roland Berry thinks it's girlie to do rollerblading."

"But we don't care," Leo informed us proudly. Then they shot off through the back door. It amazed me how they mastered steps and gravel and hills and other hazards, but they invariably did. They were strange, the twins. Nothing bothered them. They just went careering through life without looking from left to right. I sighed and went out to the shed to feed the rats. While I was in the garden I could hear Hairy doing that awful crying thing that he'd done the other day. I decided to go and see him because, after all, I'd need him to take to Sally's.

I went round to Mrs Stone's and knocked on the back door, which was opened a moment later by a very frazzled Mrs Stone.

"I was just about to phone you. I don't know what's the matter with Kenneth, but he's definitely not himself. He absolutely refuses to touch his food. When are you going to take him to the vet?"

It was on my lips to reply that I never wanted to set eyes on the vet again when I realized it wouldn't be necessary to say that. I could pretend I was taking him to the vet while actually going to Sally's eight-to-elevens class. After all, it was obvious there was nothing wrong with Hairy. He was just pining for me.

"That's what I came about actually, Mrs Stone. I'm going at ten o'clock."

"Oh good, because as you can see, he's in a complete state."

She moved slightly then and I saw that Hairy was lying under the table. I bent down and said "Hairy. Here, Hairy. Here, boy!" But apart from a slight wagging of the tail there was no reaction at all. Oh, dear! This wouldn't help me get the part of Annie, would it? I'd no idea why Hairy wasn't bounding over to meet me, but I felt sure that it was just a phase and he'd come round soon.

"I'll take him now, if you want. He'll soon liven up if he comes to play in our garden with me for a bit."

Mrs Stone looked doubtful but said I could take him and told me that, of course, she would pay the vet's fees. I hadn't thought about that. I decided I'd think about it later.

As Hairy, complete with lead that used to belong to Mrs Stone's previous dog, trundled along after me at about one mile an hour, Mrs Stone watched me through narrowed eyes.

"You're not eating enough, young lady," she suddenly remarked.

"Yes, of course I am," I smiled brightly.

"You look pale and thin. Are you ill?"

"I'm … not a hundred per cent…" That was a good phrase. I must remember that one. I'd heard adults using that expression a lot, and now she'd said I was pale I could also say I was "a bit off colour". But right now I wanted to fling my arms round her and kiss her. Mrs Stone had called me "thin"!

"Do you really think I look thin?" I asked, holding my stomach in even more and stretching up just a little to give the impression of even greater thinness.

"It's nothing to be proud of," came the forth-right answer. I went pink. I must be more careful in the future not to show that I *wanted* to be thin.

"You looked a lot better when you were normal, you know."

I yanked on Hairy's lead. I'd had enough of this conversation, and of Mrs Stone's silly grown-up opinion. "Come on, Hairy. See you later, Mrs Stone."

"I'll be here. And don't spare the pennies,

Lucy. If Kenneth needs expensive treatment, I can afford it."

"But what if someone turns up to claim him?" I couldn't help asking. After all, it was one thing being generous, but it was stupid to squander your money on something that wasn't even yours to keep.

"I think someone would have come forward by now, if anyone was going to."

There was no way Hairy was going to play in the garden. He didn't seem to have any energy at all, and neither did I. Perhaps he really was ill? No, he couldn't suddenly be ill, just like that. It was obviously just that he was hungry. It occurred to me that I hadn't asked Mrs Stone if he was off his food permanently or just today, so I nipped back to her place, leaving Hairy in the garden.

"I forgot to ask if he's been eating normally, apart from today?"

"Oh, yes, the vet will want to know that sort of thing. No, he's not eaten since I've had him, apart from a tiny bit of gravy."

I felt something wet on my hand and looked down to see Hairy at my side. He must have followed just behind me.

"He's definitely missing you, you know," Mrs Stone commented with her head on one side.

I secretly thought that was stupid because you

don't go off your food just because you're missing someone, do you?

"He's got no other symptoms of any sort, you see," she went on.

"Come on, then," I said, bending down to give Hairy a friendly pat, and sure enough he followed me back. That was a good sign for later. I needed Hairy on top form when I was demonstrating my *Annie* song to Sally.

"What are you doing with that dog back here?" Mum called through the kitchen window. Normally she would have asked me really snappily, but she was still in her let's-all-treat-Luce-like-a-fragile-package mode. Should I say I was taking him to the vet? No, she might offer to take me in the car. On the other hand, if I said I was taking him to Sally's, it might come out in front of Mrs Stone. The vet's it would have to be.

"I'm taking him to the vet's. He's off his food, apparently."

"Oh, I can easily take Mrs Stone and Hairy in the car. I'm sure she'd like to be there if he's going to see the vet."

"No, it's all arranged now, Mum. Anyway, I feel like a walk."

"Are you sure? I thought you were ill."

"I'm well enough to walk, and the fresh air'll do me good."

"Well, come and have some breakfast first."

"I don't really feel like anything, Mum."

"Either you eat something or I take you to the doctor's. Which is it going to be?" she flung at me unexpectedly, changing her tune dramatically.

"Stop overreacting, Mum…" As I said this I suddenly remembered I'd got the other famine form. "Actually, the thing is, Mum, I'm on a famine in aid of the Down's Syndrome Association, only I didn't mention it before because I didn't think you'd approve."

"Famine? Why a famine, for goodness' sake?"

"Because you have to get people to sponsor you not to eat for twenty-four hours, and all the money you get goes to the Down's Syndrome charity."

"I wish you'd just told me that, Luce, instead of pretending you're ill. You're right, I don't approve of girls of your age starving themselves, but I'd still rather know what you're up to. So when did the twenty-four hours start?"

"This morning when I got up."

"So how come you didn't eat yesterday evening, then?"

I'd forgotten about that.

"Because I really didn't feel like eating then, you see."

"Well, then surely you can count that as part of your twenty-four hours?"

"No, it's got to be all day today. That's the rule."

Mum's eyes were flashing warning signs at me.

I knew this expression on her face. She was about to go spare. She broke into one of her "I'm the boss, and this is what I say" speeches. "Go and get the form. I will add my signature to the others, but you must finish this ridiculous exercise at six o'clock this evening. Got that?"

I nodded because it was obvious she meant business, and as I turned to go and get the form I felt all dizzy, so I put my hand to my head and pretended I'd got an itch. Hairy didn't follow me upstairs but he was waiting behind the kitchen door when I got back. I'd had to write in a few names on the form in different handwritings to make it look authentic, and Mum added her signature after briefly reading the top of the form.

At ten o'clock Hairy and I went into the hall where Sally did her classes, to find about twenty eight-to-eleven-year-olds all gawping at us as though we'd just arrived from another planet or something. They'd all been chatting and mucking about while Sally was poring over a book with her back to them – the usual pre-class type of atmosphere – but my arrival caused a curious silence to work its way round, and, of course, it eventually got to Sally, too.

She turned round, saw me, smiled then frowned, then smiled again. I could tell it was an effort the second time.

"Hello, Lucy. What, er…?" She was talking to me but her eyes were on Hairy.

"Can I have a word with you?" I asked, approaching her.

"Yes, of course," she agreed. "Just talk amongst yourselves," she tossed at the class, but, of course, they didn't, because they wanted to hear what I was going to say.

I spoke in my softest voice. "I know you don't think I'd be right for Annie, Sally, but I was wondering if I could just sing you the song 'Tomorrow' with my dog, Hairy. He follows me everywhere I go, you see."

I could tell Sally was about to say no, but then she sighed and said, "Go on then, Lucy, as you're determined to show me."

She clapped her hands and got the class to sit down, which they did without any fuss because they were all obviously bursting with curiosity. I vaguely knew a few of them but I didn't feel like smiling because all of a sudden I felt ridiculously nervous. Nervousness wasn't a thing I usually felt, so it came as quite a shock to me and that made me feel even more nervous. I bent down and stroked Hairy to give myself time to collect myself. As I was stroking him I stared at a little mark on the front of the stage and thought hard about the song and about the film of *Annie* which I'd seen three times.

Whenever I am about to act or sing in a role I always get myself focused by staring at something. My heart was beating pretty fast and I hoped my voice wouldn't wobble. Sally was at the tape recorder putting in the cassette of the accompaniment that Leah had done for me ages ago when I first got interested in Annie.

I stood up and felt that same dizzy thing again but tried to ignore it. "Come on, Hairy," I said, walking a few paces to check he was following me, but he wasn't. He was just lying down, watching me. "Come on, Hairy," I repeated, slightly more urgently, as I moved off a little more quickly. There were a few giggles from the class, which irritated me because I didn't want the atmosphere spoilt. "Hairy?" whispered one grinning girl loudly to her friend. "What a weird name!"

Hairy wasn't playing. It made me feel anger welling up.

"Sorry – he's not been all that well. I'll just call him… Hang on…" I rambled. Sally looked at her watch. Oh God, I was wasting her time!

"Hairy!" I called, in a rather strained voice, patting my knees and bending forwards. He was about six metres away and he wouldn't come. He just kept watching me.

"Just sing the song, Lucy. I'm sure we can all imagine the dog's part."

She'd said that in a mocking sort of way and it

put her *with* the class, and *against* me, which really bugged me. All the same, I had no choice. This was my only chance to get this part and I had to get on with it, so I stood still and took a deep breath.

My voice, when I began, sounded a bit quavery and although it got steadily stronger it never sounded quite as it usually did. I used every ounce of energy I had to try to become Annie and felt that I was doing fairly well, but somehow it wasn't my best, no matter how hard I tried. I came to the end of the song and everyone clapped. Sally clapped and said, "Terrific... That's great, Lucy..." Then she called me over to her. This time, nobody listened. The class started chatting and went back to the way they'd been when I'd first appeared. I'd done my bit. I wasn't a mystery any more, I was just another boring person who could sing, but not brilliantly.

"You sang it beautifully, Lucy, but it's like I said the other day, it wouldn't be appropriate..." She suddenly changed tack. "I can't understand you. I've offered you the best part in *Blood Brothers*, and you don't appear to be interested."

I looked down because I didn't know what to say. It was nothing to do with *Blood Brothers*. I just wanted to do *Annie*, that was all. She patted me rather awkwardly on the back and thanked me for troubling to come specially, then said she really ought to get on, and advised me to go home and think about the part of Mrs Johnson ready for Wednesday's class. Her speech over, she was already turning to her class, clapping her hands and ordering them to their places for a dance number. So I wandered out, feeling a great weight in the pit of my stomach and in my legs.

It wasn't until I was about twenty metres away that I remembered Hairy. I turned round and there he was, right behind me.

"Why didn't you do that in there?" I demanded of him angrily.

His eyes looked bleakly up at me and his tail wagged rather pathetically.

"If it hadn't been for you, I might have got the part, you know," I went on, still eyeballing him.

I turned on my heel and walked quickly, then. I'd got it into my head that it was Hairy's fault that I'd not got the part of Annie, and I wanted to punish him so I walked as fast as I could, knowing that he would find it difficult to keep up. I was right. Turning round a minute later I saw that the distance between him and me had widened, so I waited, but with very bad grace.

Thinking that it would be a bit soon to go back home, I thought about where to go to kill a bit of time. My first thought was Jaimini's, but I quickly dismissed that because Jaimini wouldn't want to see me and anyway I didn't particularly want to see her. Then I thought of Tash. She would probably act as though nothing had happened because she was always nice, Tash was. All the same, I didn't really want anyone being nice to me, and, anyway, her mum might offer me something to eat and I couldn't be bothered to stand there making excuses. It was too much effort.

At that moment I suddenly remembered Mrs Gadsby. Well, to be precise, I thought of Mrs Gadsby's eyes. There was nothing unusual about that, because the picture of her eyes levelled at mine over the biscuit tin had flashed through my mind hundreds of times since I'd picked up the rats the other day. Goodness knows why. The only trouble with going to Mrs Gadsby's was I'd have the same problem that I'd have at Tash's, or anywhere else for that matter. I'd have to make up excuses for not eating.

Then I remembered the famine. Of course – the perfect excuse. I felt inside my pocket, but the form wasn't there. No wonder. Mum had kept it when she'd signed it. Oh well, I'd just have to explain. I didn't actually need the form to prove it, did I? A happy feeling spread through my body at that point because I'd suddenly realized that I could use an imaginary famine as an excuse not to eat whenever I wanted.

A few minutes later I was sitting in Mrs Gadsby's kitchen. A big smile had appeared on her face when she'd seen me on the doorstep. The smile had grown when she'd seen Hairy.

"Hello again! Come in… You haven't got a problem with the rats, have you?" Her face clouded over slightly then.

"Oh, no," I assured her quickly. "I just thought I'd … come and see you." It sounded stupid, but she seemed really pleased. In fact, it made her go off at about sixty miles an hour, hardly pausing for breath.

"Oh, that is *so* sweet of you. I'll make some hot chocolate and get the cake out. Don't worry, it's not coconut this time. You see, I remembered! That's right. You sit there. I can't tell you how lovely it is to see you. I don't know about you, but I always think people should drop in on other people – you know, impromptu – more often. After all, it's people knowing people that makes the world go round, isn't it? And who have you brought to see me? You're a beautiful old fellow, aren't you?" She bent down and patted Hairy and stroked his head, putting her own head close to his. She really was crazy about animals. "I hope you *are* a fellow, otherwise I shouldn't be calling you that, should I?" She finally stopped talking and looked up at me for confirmation that Hairy was indeed a fellow.

"Yes, it's a boy," I said. She was in front of the cupboard, opening the door, and I wanted to tell her about the famine, but I couldn't get a word in edgeways.

"So, how are those two rats behaving themselves? Have you noticed the difference? Well, you must have done. One so quiet and one so excitable. What have you called them?"

By this time the cake was on the table and she was going off for a knife.

"Zonc and Zinc, but I can't eat anything," I said, quickly.

"Zonc!"

"Yes," I smiled.

"And Zinc!"

"Yes." Another smile.

She had returned with the knife. It was hovering over the cake.

"I'm doing this famine, you see. It's in aid…"

"You must eat, Lucy. Your brain needs it and your body needs it," she said, in an altogether different tone. You could hardly tell that this was the same person talking. Her voice was very low and slow and gentle.

"I *do* eat normally – just not today."

I could tell she didn't believe me. But I couldn't work out how on earth she could tell. I mean, she hardly knew me!

"All right, just have a cup of hot chocolate. Just to please me. Because drinks don't count, do they?"

"We're only allowed water, really."

"All right, we'll make that a cup of tea. The amount of milk in that is next to nothing."

I nodded and felt my shoulders relaxing because we were over the worst bit.

Chapter 7

Mrs Gadsby coaxed Hairy into eating a couple of biscuits. She also tried to get him to lie down next to her, but he wouldn't. He stayed practically glued to my feet, the stupid hound.

"So, you were out on a walk, were you?" she asked me conversationally, and before I knew it I found myself telling her about the drama class and Sally and *Blood Brothers* and *Annie*. I didn't tell her everything, just concentrated on the unfairness of not being able to be Annie. I was waiting for her to make some remark like, "Ah well, that's life. We don't always get what we want, do we?" or something like that, but she didn't say anything. She just sat there listening and nodding, and every so often she murmured "Mmm". Her eyes were sort of mesmerizing me. I could have stayed there all day long, just talking to Mrs Gadsby while she said "Mmm".

After about forty minutes, I thought I ought to go because she probably had things to get on with. I thanked her for the tea and she asked me to pop back one day after school during the next week. She said not on Monday, though, because she wouldn't be in, but any other day would be fine.

Hairy came ambling after me as usual, but I was still cross with him for ruining my chances at Annie.

"How did you get on?" Mum asked, as I appeared round the back where she was weeding, with the twins blading around loudly.

I'd quite forgotten to prepare anything to say about the vet's so it had to come off the top of my head.

"Oh, OK. He said there wasn't really anything the matter. Hairy's probably adjusting to his new surroundings and just needs a bit of time. He said to come back in a week if he's not showing any signs of improvement."

I knew instantly that I'd been convincing, because Mum had returned to her weeding almost as soon as I'd begun my answer.

"You'd better go and tell Mrs Stone. She's probably worrying about him."

At that moment Mrs Stone turned up in our garden. She must have been listening out from *her* garden and heard me talking.

"What did the vet say?" she asked.

I repeated what I'd just told Mum, and she nodded and looked relieved. Mum offered Mrs Stone a cup of coffee and she accepted. I thought Mum was probably hoping she'd say no, because I know Mum, and she loves gardening but is always complaining that she doesn't get enough time for it.

Hairy seemed to liven up a tiny bit then. The twins stopped blading and played chase the stick with him. I can't say he was the fastest retriever in the world, but at least he joined in. The only time when he wouldn't play was when I went into the house and he began to follow me.

"He's obsessed with you, Luce," Leo commented.

"You must smell of girl dogs," was Tim's grubby contribution.

"Oh, shut up!" I said, because I couldn't think of anything more original to say. "I'm just going to try Terry, Mum."

"Yes, do," she encouraged me, with a bright smile.

I took the phone upstairs, sat on my bedroom floor leaning against the bed, tapped in Terry's mobile number, and waited with my knees bunched up to my chin as it rang. I didn't have to wait for long and I felt a lovely surge of happiness as Terry's voice came on.

"Hi, Terry, it's me."

"Hello! How's my favourite girl?"

"Oh, OK. Do you know when you're coming home?"

Lots of crackles came on the line then and I bunched my knees up even tighter because I didn't want the line to break up. *Stupid mobile phones!* I thought fiercely.

"I can't hear you, Terry, but if you can hear me can you phone me back? I want to talk to you."

The crackles continued but I did hear Terry's voice amongst them, though I couldn't make out what he was saying.

"Did you hear that?" I yelled down the phone.

"Yes," he replied, then there was a huge great crackle, then silence. I pressed the button to finish the call and sat there for another five minutes, waiting for Terry to ring back. As time went on, I felt more and more miserable. After all, Terry had said that he'd heard me. He knew I wanted him to ring me back, and I didn't believe there wasn't an ordinary phone handy that he could call me from. I thought he cared about me, but I was obviously wrong. My throat felt tight and a few tears dripped down my face. I happened to catch sight of myself in the mirror at that moment, which depressed me even more, because I looked all blotchy and my hair just hung like curly hay around my stupid, ugly face.

After another five minutes, my low spirits were replaced by anger and I splashed cold water all over my face and went back down to the garden. Hairy was right outside the back door, facing it, so that I practically fell over him as I went outside.

"What a stupid place to park yourself," I muttered angrily, then, "Where's Mum and Mrs Stone?" I called to my obnoxious little brothers.

"In the shed, looking at the rats," answered Leo.

I went in there out of curiosity more than anything, because the last thing I expected Mum and Mrs Stone to be doing was showing an interest in a pair of rats. The scene that met my eyes was gobsmacking, to say the least.

Mum was stroking Zonc and Mrs Stone was stroking Zinc, or was it the other way round? This was the most amazing thing of all: I couldn't tell which rat was which because both of them were so docile. I went closer and looked at the fur near their tails and saw that I'd been right. Mrs Stone was having some kind of weird calming effect on Zinc. What a joke! There was I trying to show off to Steve about how I could calm down even the most boisterous rat, and here was Mrs Stone actually *doing* it!

"Mrs Stone never knew she liked rats until this moment," Mum told me chirpily, "and neither did *I*!"

"I'd heard that they were supposed to be good pets but I'd never really believed it, you see," Mrs Stone explained. "Here, do you want to hold this one?" she offered, holding Zinc out for me to take.

"It's OK, you carry on," I replied quickly. "I can hold them any time."

Again I felt that wet nose on my hand and saw that it was disciple Hairy.

"Well, I'll let you get on, Melanie," Mrs Stone continued, talking to Mum. She popped Zinc back in his cage and Mum did the same with Zonc, then they both did this gooey *bye bye, my little gorgeous ones* sort of speech, before leaving the shed.

"Come any time," Mum invited Mrs Stone. "Even if we're not here, the shed is usually open and the rats'd be pleased to have some company, I'm sure."

Mrs Stone looked genuinely happy with this offer and said she'd definitely be taking Mum up on it. Then she called, rather off-handedly I thought, to "Kenneth" as she went home. Hairy didn't move a muscle and in the end, after several failed attempts to get him moving, I had to go back with Mrs Stone. Sure enough, the stubborn thing came then. I went into Mrs Stone's kitchen with her and we did the same routine as the last time where I quickly nipped out and pulled the door shut before Hairy could follow me. Once again, as I went I could hear him crying, but all I could think was *serves you right*.

By two-thirty that afternoon, I was so bored I decided to walk into Cableden and maybe subtly peer into the café and see who was there. I knew it was Leah's turn to work, and I thought the others might be in there, too. If they *were*, I wouldn't go in, but if there was anyone else in there who I knew well enough to sit with I'd go in, and just ignore Leah. Otherwise I'd have to wander round Cableden and look in shop windows. Terry hadn't phoned back and I was utterly fed up.

I approached the café cautiously and walked slowly past it, glancing in the window as subtly as I could, but also as thoroughly as I could, to try to see with only one look who was there. I didn't think it would be particularly cool to have to walk past going in the other direction while peering in.

The very first person I saw was Tash. She was beckoning me frantically and smiling for all she was worth. She was sitting with Fen, so I decided that maybe I'd go and join them. At least Jaimini and Andy weren't there.

"Hi! We wondered if you'd come along," Tash greeted me warmly.

Does anything make her mad? I thought, with irritation.

126

Fen had obviously been briefed by Tash to be nice to me, but she wasn't finding it very easy. Tash got straight on to the subject of the rats, which I thought was quite daring of her. So did Fen, judging from the look on her face when Tash spoke.

"If I were you I'd just go right up to Jan and apologize about the rats, Luce, otherwise you're going to have it hanging over you for ages. There'll also be a bad atmosphere between you two every time you're in here."

"It wasn't me who left the cage door open, you know," I snapped back at her, and that made Fen's hackles rise.

"Tash is just trying to be helpful," she said rather aggressively. "The least you can do is be grateful."

"It's OK, Fen," Tash quickly interrupted her friend, then she turned to me again. "Look, we know you're upset, and you're probably upset about Terry being away too..."

"Oh, do me a favour and drop the amateur psychologist bit," I cut in, because it made me so cross the way she sounded so patronizing.

Again Fen sprang to her friend's defence.

"What you call 'the amateur psychologist bit' is Tash being kind and thoughtful, and trying to think of reasons to excuse you being so totally off your trolley at the moment!"

I didn't have to answer that because Leah appeared. I had to admit it was quite a relief to see her at that moment because I wasn't quite sure *how* to answer Fen. It wasn't that I thought she was right, just that she'd dressed up the truth very cleverly, and my brain wasn't as quick as hers.

"Would you like something to drink?" Leah asked me quietly.

"Tea, please," I answered, with an attempt at a smile.

"Tea!"

"Yeah, tea. It's a drink quite commonly served in cafés, you know," I went on sarcastically.

Leah blushed and quickly scribbled on her pad, while Fen stood up, pushing her chair back noisily, and went off in the direction of the loos. It was obvious she'd had enough of me. As soon as she'd gone Tash tried again.

"What's the matter, Luce? *Please* tell me. I'm so worried about you, and I can't stand it when people aren't getting on with each other."

I looked at her big brown eyes and wished there was something I could tell her, but there wasn't. There were only two things wrong with me. One: I was missing Terry, and two: I wished I could have the part of Annie. Goodness knows why everybody thought I was ill, or that there was something the matter with me when there wasn't.

As it happened I was saved from answering Tash's question because the door opened and who should come in but Steve. Tash's eyes darted straight to the door, presumably because she'd seen the look of alarm on my face. Then immediately afterwards Jan walked past me and gave me a long, searching look but didn't even speak.

I sighed and said, "I don't know what I'm doing here. It's perfectly obvious I'm not wanted."

Steve saw me at that moment and gave me a curt nod.

"I agree you wouldn't win the Miss Popularity of the Year Award," Tash said, smiling cheekily, "but don't make it any worse on yourself, Luce."

That was quite witty for Tash, and I had a job not grinning. But I didn't want to give her the satisfaction of thinking she was getting through to me. I wanted to stay as I was – ungetthroughable-to. Yes, that was it, I didn't want anyone trying to be too friendly with me until I'd cracked my diet. I'd decided I just had to get down to six-stone-ten, then I'd be OK. I'd be thin and confident, and I wouldn't need to turn down food any more.

"How's Hairy?" Steve said, drawing up a chair at our table.

It was funny, but when I looked at him now he

didn't seem at all attractive. He just made me sick for making a fool out of me over the rats. Leah appeared with my tea and took Steve's order, but I didn't feel even one gramme of jealousy like I'd felt before, because it wasn't important any more.

"Not very well," I answered Steve's question rather huffily.

"So why haven't you made an appointment to come and see me?" he came straight back at me.

"Because I don't think I'd be very welcome," I replied, bolshily.

"Oh, for goodness' sake, Lucy," he went on, lowering his voice and leaning forwards. "I'm not so unprofessional that I harbour personal grievances and take them into the surgery with me. If your dog is ill, bring him in on Monday. I can tell you straight away that I'm free at six o'clock. Now, don't forget... Ah, here's Donna." He smiled and waved at Donna as she came in, then got up to go and meet her. I looked the other way because I didn't want to have to acknowledge her.

Jaimini and Andy came in then, and I really started to feel hemmed in. I was surrounded by people who didn't like me – apart from Tash, and she was only making an effort because she hates trouble. I was on the point of standing up to go when Leah came back for the third time and told us what Jan had just told her. Jaimini and Andy came straight over to our table and tuned into what Leah was saying immediately, without even saying hello.

"Jan says that on Monday there's a Down's Syndrome Association committee meeting in here. There'll be all sorts of people who are involved with Down's Syndrome coming to the meeting. It's to talk about how they're going to spend the money they've raised at recent events apparently, so Jan's shutting the café from three-thirty till five-thirty, so they can all have tea in peace. She said to tell you all in case we were thinking of coming in after school."

"It's my turn to work on Monday, but I was going to ask if anyone else could do it because I'm babysitting Peta," Tash said. There was a brief silence, then Jaimini, who hadn't even said hello to me, said, "Why don't you do it, Luce? You're interested in Down's Syndrome, aren't you? Wasn't that what your famine was in aid of?"

I looked at her and immediately thought she was being sarcastic. She'd sussed me and my not-eating campaign. I bet she'd discussed it with the others and they'd all agreed I was a big liar and not to be trusted. The way she came out with it just like that made me really mad, but I wasn't going to give her the satisfaction of knowing that, so I just said, "Yeah, I'll do it, Tash."

"Oh, great, and I'll do yours on Wednesday,"

Tash said happily, which worked out perfectly because of drama club.

Then I stood up, handed Leah the money for my tea, said bye to anyone who might have been listening and went. I could feel them staring at me as I walked over to the door. There were five pairs of eyes all boring into my back. I stood up straight and hoped they could see how thin I was getting.

If I look back now on those few days and the next two, the main thing I remember about them is that they were so lonely. Terry did phone back, but it was on the Saturday afternoon and I was out. I ate something resembling a very small meal on Saturday night with Mum watching my every move. I hated every mouthful of it and wished I could be sick after it.

All day Sunday I just flopped around doing nothing really. I refused to eat at Sunday lunch-time, and when I refused the evening meal, too, Mum said, "Right, that's it, I'm taking you to the doctor's tomorrow after school."

"But I'm working in the café, and then I'm taking Hairy to the vet's."

The moment the words were out of my mouth I realized my mistake.

"But you only took him to the vet's yesterday."

I must have gone pink because Mum was at me

like a shot. "Or was that *not* what you did on Saturday?"

I didn't answer, and I could positively *feel* Mum's helpless exasperation. "I'll be glad when Terry gets back. I don't know where I am with you these days, Lucy."

"So will I be glad, then maybe I'll get some peace from *you*," I snapped, and slammed out of the room. I didn't care any more about hiding the fact that I wasn't eating. It would be impossible to hide it for much longer anyway, so I might as well just keep refusing to eat. She couldn't *make* me eat after all, and even if she made me go to the doctor's, *he* couldn't make me, either. I knew Terry wouldn't make me. I was his little girl.

On Monday morning when I weighed myself it said six-stone-thirteen. I did the hands round waist test and found that my thumbs were even closer. I didn't feel particularly well, though, and I really didn't want to go to school, partly because of the others being there, but mainly because of having to get through lunchtime. Now that Mum knew I wasn't going to eat anything except the tiniest bit if I *had* to, it was much easier to stay at home.

"I'm not well enough to go to school," I told Mum, as I sipped a lemon tea, while the twins scoffed Weetabix with honey and sultanas.

"I'm taking you to the doctor's," she informed me briefly.

"What if I refuse to go?" I replied calmly.

She looked frightened when I said that. There was no other word for it. I had definitely made her frightened. Good, because she needed to know who was boss.

"Then I'll get the doctor to come here," she answered.

"What if I'm not here when the doctor comes?" I counter-attacked.

She didn't answer, just pursed her lips and started tidying up. The twins were silent for once, looking from me to Mum and back again with big, stary eyes.

"What's the matter with Lucy?" Leo whispered to Mum at the sink.

"Nothing for you to worry about," Mum answered lightly. "Come on, you two, chop chop. Get your school stuff together."

She was trying to be all brisk and normal to show the twins there wasn't anything wrong. She never mentioned the doctor again, but she didn't walk the twins to school like she usually did, she got another mother to come and collect them. She obviously didn't trust me not to run away.

"I think you'd better get one of your friends to work at the café today. If you're not well enough for school, then you're not well enough to go to work, that's for sure."

"I'm perfectly well enough for the café. I only

spend two hours there, whereas school is from quarter to nine until quarter to four, which is miles longer."

Again, Mum pursed her lips but didn't reply. I noticed that she kept looking at her watch, and I wondered why. Perhaps she *was* expecting the doctor, although when she could have arranged that I didn't know because she hadn't made any phone calls to my knowledge.

At about two–thirty, when I was lounging on the settee reading a comic of Leo's, Mum suddenly came into the sitting room, and right behind her was Terry! I leapt up, but felt dizzy and flopped back again.

"*Omigod!*" were Terry's first words. "What *have* you been doing to yourself? You can't even stand up!"

He just stood there. Didn't smile, didn't give me a big bear hug like he normally did, just stood there and stared at me, and he'd been away all that time and couldn't even greet me properly. But worse than that, he hadn't even noticed how lovely and slim I was. I couldn't believe it! Then to make matters even worse, he'd come home early and Mum hadn't bothered to tell me she was expecting him. I would have been at school if I'd been fit enough to go. She made me sick. They both did.

With a big effort I got to my feet again, and this

time my anger gave me energy. I bolted past the still stunned-looking Terry into the hall, out of the front door, down the street and round the first corner I came to, without slowing to less than a jog at any point. At first I didn't know where I was going. All I wanted was to get away from the look in Terry's eyes, then when I realized that nobody had followed me, I slowed down and began to think where I ought to go. I finally settled on the library because I could sit down there and read something, and no one would think of looking for me in there, either. Then, at four o'clock I'd go to the café and by that time, Mum and Terry would have calmed down a bit, with any luck.

It took me ages to get to the library, because I'd set off in completely the wrong direction when I was trying to get away from home as quickly as possible. Once I was finally there, I sat down in a big easy chair in the corner and curled up with a book, but I couldn't concentrate because pictures kept crowding into my mind all the time.

Pictures of Steve looking daggers at me, Donna crying, Tash looking compassionate, the twins looking big-eyed, Mum looking frightened, Terry looking stunned, but most of all, Mrs Gadsby with that all-knowing, all-seeing gaze. I don't know why that picture should keep coming into my mind, but it did, and I suddenly made a decision. I would go and see Mrs Gadsby. Mrs Gadsby would make me feel better. She did the last time. And she *had* told me to go and see her one day after school.

Then I remembered, Mrs Gadsby had said she'd be out on Monday, and suddenly it was as though the whole world was conspiring against me. It was quarter to four, so I decided to set off for the café, and then the pictures would stop coming because I'd be working.

It was probably the slowest walk I'd ever done because I had so little energy. I pushed open the kitchen door and Kevin stopped mid-song and stared at me.

"Should … you … be here?" he asked, slowly.

"Yeah, it's my turn. I swapped with Tash…"

"No, I mean, are you well enough?"

"I'm just a bit off colour, that's all," I told him on my way through to the café. Then I went through the swing door and stopped in my tracks because the place was silent, except for one voice. People were sitting round the tables all looking towards the speaker, who had their undivided attention.

And the speaker was Mrs Gadsby.

Chapter 8

Jan was standing on the other side of the café, listening intently with her head on one side and a little smile on her face. She glanced over when she heard the door open, and immediately put her finger to her lips to tell me to keep quiet. Nobody else looked around. They were all too wrapped up in what Mrs Gadsby was saying. I got the impression she'd only just started speaking because she was saying what a wonderful period it had been and what a fantastic sum of money had been raised. She went on to list all the various ways in which the money was going to be spent.

As I listened, I could feel myself getting involved with what Mrs Gadsby was saying in the same way that everyone else obviously was. Then she set up a projector – there was already a screen behind her – and announced that she was going to show a short film about Down's Syndrome children, after which tea would be served. So the film started and as it rolled, Mrs Gadsby talked about the various scenes.

First we saw a school, an ordinary primary school, then the film took us inside one of the classrooms and we could see all the tables in little clusters with small children around them. The camera focused on a little girl called Sam who was a Down's Syndrome child. She had fair hair tied back in a ponytail, very thick glasses, and small eyes set close together. Her face wasn't pretty at all but when she smiled she looked adorable. Her cheeks were chubby and her mouth seemed to be permanently open, especially when she was concentrating. Her nose was continually running and she kept rubbing her hand over it. She couldn't concentrate for very long at a time, and there was a woman who was obviously there solely to look after her.

Every so often Sam would plant a sloppy kiss on her helper's cheek or give her a big hug, and I thought what a sweet, loving child she was. She also hugged the other children in the class, and though she looked and acted so very differently from them, they all accepted her.

We saw snippets of Sam in a music and movement class, then in a drama class and an art class, and lastly in a PE class. She kept waving at the camera and every time she did that a little ripple of laughter went round the café.

"They're all like that, Down's Syndrome children – full of love and affection," one woman sitting near me whispered to her friend.

My legs were feeling tired by then, but there was nowhere for me to sit, except in the kitchen, and I didn't want to miss the film so I leaned against the wall. Jan glanced over at me again and frowned. She looked as though she was thinking of mouthing something to me across the room, but changed her mind. She didn't smile and neither did I.

After a few more minutes spent following Sam to the canteen and watching her eat her lunch, that bit finished, and the film went on to show a community college. Here the Down's Syndrome children were much older, in fact some of them were adults. Their bodies were big and solid-looking, but they weren't very tall which made them look even heavier. Their faces were much fuller and more rounded than most people's, but none of this stopped me from thinking that they were lovely people.

Mrs Gadsby spoke about them as the film rolled. She obviously knew a lot of them personally and spoke with great affection about them. There were loads of helpers in the centre and they were all very patient, kind people. Some of them were women and some men. After a few minutes of general scenes, the camera focused in on a boy, or it could have been a man. It's very difficult to tell how old Down's Syndrome people are, because their faces are very smooth and open-looking, and because they're so small yet stocky. I guessed the person on the film was about twenty.

"This is Charlie," Mrs Gadsby was saying, and again a little murmur went round the café. It wasn't like the ripple of laughter the last time. This was more like a murmur of sympathy. Everybody obviously knew who Charlie was. I felt as though I ought to know, too. Where had I heard that name recently? We saw Charlie doing woodwork and doing drawing, then making something with clay.

After that, some music started on the film and there was no talking at all. Mrs Gadsby didn't talk either for a little while. All this next part was of close ups of Charlie reacting to different things he was watching, so we saw him clap his hands over his mouth as he laughed at a clown on TV, then we saw him looking very serious and frowning at a computer screen, next we saw him with a big scowl on his face because he obviously didn't like the look of whatever was on his plate at lunchtime. After that, were several shots of Charlie with a girl or a woman of about the same age as him. Mrs Gadsby did just say at that moment that this was Bella, Charlie's girlfriend.

Again that murmur went round the café. But there was a total stillness and silence around me as the next picture came on the screen, still with the music in the background. It was of Charlie and Bella hugging each other and rocking backwards and forwards. The camera went first to Charlie's face and we saw that he had tears in his eyes, then to Bella's face and we saw that she was happy and smiling.

"Bella didn't have any idea that Charlie was about to be taken from her," said Mrs Gadsby softly, "but I think Charlie knew he didn't have long to go."

At that point I noticed one lady watching wipe a tear from her face. Then the film showed Bella sitting on a swing in a garden. She wasn't swinging, she was just sitting looking down, and the camera very slowly went closer and closer until we could see that she was crying. I could feel my throat hurting and my own eyes watering as I watched. I could hardly bear it, it was so sad.

The film ended there, and Mrs Gadsby looked up and said, "Charlie died two days later, but Bella is still grieving, even now, three months later. Fortunately, she's in a place where she's surrounded by love and plenty of stimulating things to do and that's where all this money that you've all helped to raise comes in…"

She was still talking, but I didn't hear another word she said because something very important had dawned on me. I had suddenly realized with a massive jolt like an electric shock just who Charlie was: Charlie was Mrs Gadsby's son. That's why Mrs Gadsby was the Chairman of the Down's Syndrome Association. That's why she was standing at the front doing the speech. And Charlie used to keep rats, like his two brothers, but now *I'd* got Charlie's two rats because Mrs Gadsby didn't want them to be separated because they're brothers and they'd miss each other. And now Charlie's dead, and his brothers must be missing him dreadfully. And in a home somewhere is a poor fat ugly girl called Bella who used to love Charlie, but now she's grieving and crying because Charlie's dead.

As these thoughts went through my head, something was happening in my mind, something was falling into place. That electric shock had jolted my senses back into perspective. Those pictures in my mind were coming back. I could see Steve looking daggers at me, and Donna crying. But then something weird happened. The picture of Donna turned into one of Bella crying and that turned into Terry crying. *Terry!* I gasped.

Terry had come home early because he was so

worried about me. He had stared at me and couldn't understand why I looked so different from the stepdaughter he'd left just a few days before, and as he'd stared in horror, I had leapt up and run away from him. I had to get back – quickly! He must be so sad, so worried. My throat was so choked up it was almost unbearable.

Without a word or even a glance I swung through the door into the kitchen, ignoring Kevin's look of amazement, and went out through the back door, then ran all the way home. I was puffing and panting but I was so desperate to get back that I just ignored my aching legs and lungs. I couldn't move fast enough.

As I approached our house I could see someone standing at the gate, looking up and down the road. The figure saw me and began to run towards me. As he got closer I could see that it was Terry. Terry can't run for toffee. He's far too overweight and unfit, but he was running now all right, and so was I. He ran right up to me and scooped me up in his arms and twirled me round, keeping me tight to him, then put me down, and still without saying anything he walked me slowly back to the house with his arm round my shoulder as though he daren't let go of me completely.

In the house Mum came rushing up and put her arms round us both and burst into tears.

"Thank goodness you've come back," she said through her tears, and I tried to hug her *and* Terry, but I couldn't because I didn't have any strength left. Terry must have realized because he picked me up and carried me over to the settee. I flopped back thankfully as Terry said in a strained sort of voice, "We're going to get you better now, love."

"I wanted you to phone back," I said.

"If I'd only known…" he replied, shaking his head sadly.

"It's called anorexia, what you've got," Mum said, gently.

I'd heard of anorexia. It's where you can't eat or you don't want to eat, or both. But *I* hadn't got that. I was just on a diet. I was just trying to lose weight.

"No, Mum, I haven't got that, honestly."

"Yes, you have, love," Terry told me firmly, but just as gently. "One of the symptoms is that you don't realize you've got it."

"I've been watching a film…"

Neither Mum nor Terry commented on that, they just waited.

"It was about Down's Syndrome people … and there was this sort of boy or man called Charlie in it and his girlfriend, Bella."

"Beautiful, that means," said Terry.

"Yes… Only she wasn't beautiful. She was fat

and ugly, but she loved Charlie … and then he died."

As I spoke those words I realized I was going to cry, and cry I did. I cried and cried and cried until I had no more tears left inside me and all the while Terry hugged me and rocked me and stroked my hair. "And you thought you were fat," he finally said, with a small smile.

"I was too big for the part of Annie… *Great big*, that's what the drama teacher called me … twice. But I know she didn't really mean it. I don't think I'm fat any more." And I didn't. I felt as though my life had been a dream for the last few days and I'd just woken up and I was lucky to be alive.

"Can I have some toast, Mum?"

"Nothing would give me greater pleasure than to make you some toast," laughed Mum, as she went out to the kitchen.

"And don't you dare give us a scare like that again," Terry said, wagging his finger at me in mock temper. I grinned and when he asked jokingly if I'd be safe to leave for five minutes, I told him only five because I wanted to show him my pet rats.

"Yes, I've been hearing about these rats from your mother. I'm not sure that I'm brave enough to face rats, you know."

"Yes, you are. They're lovely. They used to

belong to Charlie." Saying Charlie's name again took me back to the café and I suddenly sat bolt upright and clapped my hand to my mouth. "Omigod! I've left Jan completely in the lurch without anyone to help her!"

So Mum phoned the café and it turned out that Becky was there with Jan, and the two of them were managing just fine. I didn't hear what Mum said to Jan because she took the phone into the other room, but whatever it was, it was a long conversation. I ate the toast very slowly and I only managed two pieces, but it was a start. Mum was keeping an eye on me and I could tell she was wishing I'd eat all four pieces.

"I can't, Mum," I told her.

"Is it because you're scared of getting fat?" she asked, carefully.

"I'll never ever feel the same again about being fat, after watching that film. You see, I know Charlie's mother. Her name is Mrs Gadsby. And she loved Charlie even though he was so fat."

"It's got nothing to do with what we look like, has it?" Mum agreed. "You love someone because – well, because you just love them."

"But what about..." I hesitated, because though I felt like talking, it was difficult to put into words how I'd felt, and how I still *did* feel a bit.

"What about fancying someone, you mean?"

Mum asked, without any expression on her face at all. I nodded.

"I think it's the same as love. I *think*. You fancy someone just because you fancy them. The point is that everybody's got different tastes, you know, different things they find attractive, but most of the attraction is for the way the person *is*, not just how they look, and definitely not how *thin* they are!"

"It's just that boys look at Leah and Jaimini more than me."

"Who's the thinnest in your group?"

"Well, I suppose it's Andy, but that's because she's little."

"Yeah, exactly, that's how she is. She's little and thin. Do boys look at her like they look at Leah?"

"Well … no."

"Does Andy starve herself to try and improve the situation?"

"No, because Andy's different. She doesn't care about all that stuff."

"Sensible girl. And because of that, when she *does* have boyfriends, she'll be absolutely sure that the attraction they feel is for the way she *is*."

I thought about this for ages and Mum didn't say any more on the subject. She'd said a lot, and I'd learnt a lot, and I knew I wasn't going to go back to normal eating straight away, but the important thing was that I'd come to my senses. I sat on that settee for ages, just thinking back over the last few days. I'd done ridiculous things, I'd done horrible things, I'd acted like a spoilt brat. It made me blush to think about it.

How I was ever going to be accepted back into the Café Club I didn't know. Jan was furious with me, and no wonder. My friends were sick of me, and my best friend didn't want to know me. As for Steve... I blushed as I thought about him. How could I have fancied someone as old as him? I made a resolution that from that moment in time, I would *only* fancy boys of my own age – well, I'd try to anyway!

Terry hated the rats. He couldn't even bring himself to hold them. Mum was showing off by stroking them and letting them run round her shoulders, then Mrs Stone suddenly appeared in the shed.

"Hello, Terry," she said, as she took one of the rats from Mum and cuddled it right up to her face. "Back from your travels?"

Terry nodded and stood back, as though he was afraid that if he stood too close, one of these reckless women might just plant a rat on him.

"How can you *do* that, Mrs Stone?" he winced.

"Because they're gorgeous," Mrs Stone answered, which made Terry shudder and tell her she must be mad.

"How's Hairy – I mean, Kenneth?" Mum asked her, sounding anxious.

"He's still off his food," replied Mrs Stone. "It's difficult to know with Kenneth, although I've said all along that I reckon he's pining for you, Lucy."

I smiled, but secretly thought he was just a loopy dog. I mean, we weren't living in a Walt Disney film, were we? Terry wanted to know what we were all talking about, so Mum did a fast explanation, then asked carefully of Mrs Stone, "Do you think he needs to go ... *back* to the vet's?"

"I expect he'll be OK for a day or two," was the answer.

Watching the look on Mrs Stone's face as she stroked the rats, it occurred to me that she'd probably prefer to keep the rats than a big, energetic dog. Then I remembered that Hairy wasn't energetic any more.

Mrs Stone was frowning and shaking her head slowly and thoughtfully.

"The trouble is, I'm worried that he's ill. I'd rather he was boisterous than like he is now. Mind you, when he *was* boisterous he used to practically knock me over. I don't know, all these years, ever since my old dog Dolly died, I've thought I wanted another dog to take her place, but it's funny, you know, I think I've changed. These little rats seem like far better company to me now, and ten years ago you'd have knocked me down with a feather if you'd said I was going to cuddle a couple of rodents!"

"I *do* think you ought to take Hairy back to the vet, you know, Luce," Mum said a bit later. It was obvious Mum was being very careful not to upset me. She was deliberately avoiding mentioning that I'd obviously been lying on Saturday and that I *hadn't* taken Hairy to the vet's. She was also probably remembering that earlier on that day, when I'd been arguing about going to school, I'd said that I was going to see the vet after working at the café.

"*I* don't want to be the one to take him, Mum. He's not my dog."

"He's not really Mrs Stone's responsibility, either," Mum said, with a frown. "In fact, I get the impression that Mrs Stone is rather regretting taking him on in the first place."

"Well, maybe his real owners will show up soon."

"That's not the point. The point is that if he's ill, it's up to us to take care of him and get him better."

"But you heard Mrs Stone. She didn't seem all that worried. She said it would be OK to leave him for a couple of days."

"All the same, if you've got an appointment for tonight…?"

It was no good. I couldn't bear to have to go and see Steve. I felt so embarrassed and ashamed.

151

"Couldn't you make an appointment for tomorrow or Wednesday, Mum, and take him yourself?" I pleaded, without actually answering the question she'd sort of asked, which was whether I'd got an appointment.

"All right," she agreed with a sigh. "I'll phone tomorrow and get an appointment for tomorrow evening or Wednesday. I've got too much to do this evening, I'm afraid."

"Thanks, Mum," I said, breathing a sigh of relief that at least I'd probably never have to set eyes on Steve again. I knew he'd be far too professional to be cross with Mum about me not turning up at six o'clock today. At last I was beginning to relax. Three problems were out of the way now. I didn't have to face Steve again, Terry was home, and best of all I didn't have to invent excuses the whole time for not eating. It was such a relief, such an enormous relief. I went straight upstairs, got the scales and put them under Mum and Terry's bed, vowing that I'd never ever stand on them again.

"All the same, Luce," Mum said, when I'd come back down, just as though our conversation had never been interrupted, "you've got to face your friends some time, you know."

I wondered how Mum knew there was anything wrong between my friends and me. Another blush was creeping up my face at the thought that Jan might have told her about the rat in the café episode. I didn't ask because I didn't want to hear the answer. I just nodded and went back upstairs.

For the next hour and a half I listened to my cassette of *Blood Brothers*, and looked through my script until I'd learnt massive great chunks of Mrs Johnson's role. I knew I'd probably spoilt my chances of getting that role now, with my stupid *I want to be Annie* display, but all the same I was going to go for it and it would serve me right if I didn't get it.

Just before I went to bed the phone rang. It was Mrs Stone to say that the police had contacted her to tell her that Kenneth or Hairy or Harry – as his real name apparently was – had been reported missing. He'd run away from a dogs' home quite a few miles away, and the people there had hesitated to contact the police because they rather hoped that he'd found a nice new home for himself. The woman who had spoken to the police officer had apparently laughed and said that she felt stupid reporting a dog missing from a home because usually she had to report that dogs had been found and *taken* to the home! She'd only phoned in the end just to check that Harry was safe and being looked after.

"You mean the dogs' home don't want Hairy back?" I asked Mum. She nodded. "Not unless nobody else wants him."

"But what's Mrs Stone going to do? She doesn't really want him, either."

"She says she's keeping him for the time being because she hasn't the heart to send him back to the dogs' home, then she's going to see if she can find a more suitable home for him. Apparently she's got a nephew with two children of eight and nine and she thinks they might like him, but first she just wants to get him better. She's coming with me to the vet's when I go."

That night I dreamt about Hairy. I dreamt he was walking slowly back to our house from Mrs Stone's nephew's house, and on the way he collapsed from exhaustion and the police picked him up and he went to live at the police station. It was a weird dream!

Chapter 9

The following morning when I woke up, my mind was immediately flooded with memories. I very nearly put my hands round my waist but I stopped myself just in time. Getting up slowly and putting on my school uniform, I thought ahead to the day at school. I was dreading it. There was no way I'd be able to get back with Jaimini and the others unless I made some sort of big apology, and I knew I'd never dare do that because of the fear that they might hate my guts even *after* that.

"I'm still not all that well, Mum…" I began, as I sat at the breakfast table eating some grapefruit and orange segments coated with honey and covered with raisins that Mum had prepared.

"One step at a time, that's what I say," Terry said.

"Well, could today's step be eating normally?" I asked.

"Yes, of course! That's a big step," said Mum, with a beam.

"Can we have Frosties, Mum?" asked Tim, after the twins had pulled gross faces at each other to express their total delight with Mum's lovingly prepared breakfast.

"Oh, go on then," Mum relented, and Terry spooned the rest of the contents of Tim's and Leo's bowls into his own and proceeded to eat his way through the whole lot.

"What I meant was, can I miss school just for one day? I still feel quite weak, you see…"

Mum and Terry exchanged suspicious looks. It was Terry who spoke.

"Look, we don't know what's been going on in your life over the last few days, and we're not asking, but whatever it is, you've got to get things back to normal. It might take a lot of courage but it's got to be done sooner or later, so why don't you tackle it sooner and get it over with?"

I knew he was right. I'd just have to get on with it. Maybe it wouldn't be as bad as I thought once I got to school.

As it turned out, it was every bit as bad. Tash was the only one of the five of them who looked as though she cared at all. Jaimini seemed to be making a point of keeping out of my way. Fen didn't even appear to notice that I existed and neither did Andy. Leah wasn't around much because she had music practices at break and lunchtime.

By then, I was feeling thoroughly fed up with the lot of them. They weren't at all sympathetic and they were supposed to be my friends, so stuff them! After lunch, Tash finally approached me with her big, worried eyes and said, "Oh, Luce, why don't you make things up with Jaimini?" and I suddenly flipped.

"Why doesn't *she* make things up with me, you mean! She doesn't even bother to find out what's the matter with me. None of you do!"

With that I stomped off, knowing that I'd killed any possible little chance there might have been of getting back together with them. As the rest of the day went on, I felt more and more miserable and isolated. What a stupid idiot I'd been! I should have gone straight up to Jaimini when Tash had approached me, and simply apologized, but now it was too late. It would be just *too* demeaning to have to apologize now, and they'd be quite within their rights to tell me to get lost and never return.

By the end of the day, I was so desperate to have my friends back and to be in the Café Club again with Jan being nice and normal, that I made a resolution. I was going to go to the café on my own and approach them all at the same time, say I was sorry, grovel like mad, and generally do whatever was necessary to make them accept me again. Having made the resolution, I felt better and all the way to the café I kept this positive feeling up.

The moment I walked through the door I realized it was Fen on duty, because the other four were sitting together all chatting and laughing at a table for four. I took a deep breath and approached them, my heart beating faster than usual and my mouth feeling dry. This was worse than stage fright, this was.

When I was almost at Jaimini's side, someone called my name, very softly and icily. I turned to see Steve at the corner table. His face was like thunder as he jerked his head at me to tell me to go over to him. The café was full of people, thank goodness, because I had the horrible feeling I was about to be shouted at. I sat down opposite Steve feeling like a naughty little kid who had to see the teacher for misbehaving.

I was wrong about the shouting, though, because Steve's voice was so low I could hardly hear him.

"Your mother brought Harry to see me today. That dog is suffering from malnutrition. It was brought on at first by wandering the streets for a couple of days, I guess, but more recently it's been as a result of neglect. It's not Mrs Stone's fault. She's an old lady and she didn't have any idea how bad the dog had got, but she's right about one thing. It's perfectly obvious to me that the dog wants to be with you. Mrs Stone's told me every detail of Harry's behaviour when you're there and when you're not there. Don't you care at all about the poor thing? You don't seem to show any interest in his welfare."

He paused at this moment and looked at me as though I was some kind of monster. I didn't say anything. I felt a bit sad about Hairy but I still didn't think it was my fault.

"Why didn't you bring him to me sooner? And why did you tell Mrs Stone you'd already brought him to me on Saturday?" He was beginning to raise his voice. "That's why the poor old lady thought he was all right, because you'd told her that I'd said he'd be fine and that he was simply readjusting to his new situation. You'd said, 'Don't worry, just take him back in a week's time if he's no better'. So naturally Mrs Stone had thought, if that's what the vet said, there can't be anything to worry about."

By this time Steve was speaking so that other people *must* have been able to hear him. I didn't dare look to right or left. I kept my blushing beet-root face right in his line of fire.

"And then to cap it all, you couldn't even be bothered to turn up yesterday evening when I'd fitted you in at very short notice and was staying on at the surgery especially for *your* visit."

From behind me I heard Andy say "Huh!", then the other three made similar disgusted noises and began whispering together as though I was a bit of dirt or something. I didn't know what to do. I felt half angry and half despairing. Steve was still eyeballing me.

"I couldn't come…" I began defending myself, knowing it was hopeless.

"What's that supposed to mean?"

"I couldn't face you…"

He didn't say anything to that, so I stood up rather unsteadily and went. I could feel tears pricking at the backs of my eyes, and I could also feel my ex-friends watching me leave. As I went past the window I took the fastest glance in the world at Steve and saw that he was sitting with his head in his hands. What a mess, what a stupid, stupid mess I'd made of everything. I couldn't go home. I didn't want Mum feeling sorry for me and trying to protect me, so without making any conscious decision about where to go, I found that my footsteps were taking me towards Mrs Gadsby's house.

"Hello, Lucy! Come in, love."

I sat down at her table and she went straight to the kettle as I knew she would, and then to the cupboard. I guessed she'd be expecting me not to eat, and I wanted to tell her that I was all right now. I was better. I could eat, but I genuinely didn't feel like it because I was too sad. As she took the lid off the cake tin, all sorts of words of explanation were beginning to form in my head to try to get her to understand that there was nothing to worry about. But it all seemed too complicated, so when the time came I meekly accepted the cake and slowly chewed my way through it, not enjoying it one bit, but noticing all the same that by eating it I was giving Mrs Gadsby enormous pleasure.

"I saw you at the café. I was working, only I didn't feel well and I had to go… But I saw the film … and … Charlie."

Her face lit up.

"You saw the film! Well, bless me! I'd no idea you were there. So now you've seen my Charlie."

Talking about him made me sad again but Mrs Gadsby didn't look sad, she looked happy to have someone to talk about him to. So I stayed for three quarters of an hour and not a single word was spoken about me. All the talk was about Charlie, which made me feel better, because every time the picture of Steve's angry face flashed into my mind, or the sound of Andy's disgusted "Huh!" came into my head, I just kept reminding myself that my position wasn't half as bad as Mrs Gadsby's. I wasn't mourning a dead relative or friend, after all.

"Do you know something?" Mrs Gadsby said, as I got up to go. "You do me more good than all the counselling in the world!"

"Counselling?" I repeated a bit dumbly.

"I go every week for counselling for bereaved parents, but it's not as good as sitting here with you." She chuckled when she said that, and that made me laugh, too.

"I've never heard you laugh, you know," she commented. "I thought you were the really serious type – very academic, always studying, you know –"

I opened my eyes wide in amazement and shook my head. "No, I'm not... I'm just serious at the moment. But I'm supposed to be the crazy one, actually."

There was a long pause after I'd spoken those words, then Mrs Gadsby let out a great, long laugh and said, "Well if you're the crazy one, I know a few people who ought to have been consigned to the loony bin long ago!" I didn't know what she meant but I laughed with her and promised to go and see her again after a few days.

"Or maybe I'll come and see you at that café? That would be nice."

I couldn't be bothered to say that I might not be going there much more, so I just smiled and agreed that that would be nice, then off I went home.

Mrs Stone and Hairy were in our living room with Mum when I walked in. I dreaded hearing what Mum would say about the visit to the vet's. She started on that subject the moment I walked in.

"The vet thinks Hairy's missing you. He's pining because he wants to be with you. That's why he's off his food."

Hairy had his back to me. His head was between his two front paws. I crouched down and called his name.

"Hairy, Hairy."

Immediately he got up, came ambling over to me and flopped down beside me.

"He's got no energy and he won't take food from me," Mrs Stone said, in a worried voice. "I've got some tablets for him but he won't take those either because they're supposed to be crunched up in his food and he won't eat anything."

"You try feeding him, Luce," Mum said.

So we all trooped over to Mrs Stone's place and I opened the can of food and spooned it into the bowl with Hairy watching my every move, then I placed it in front of him and ... absolutely nothing happened!

"The vet's talking rubbish if he thinks Hairy's pining for me," I said rather snappily. "He's just trying to make me feel guilty for…"

I suddenly realized that I had said too much. Mrs Stone was merely looking puzzled but Mum looked very suspicious. I knew she'd try to tackle me later about what my problem was with the vet. Anyway, in the meantime I'd proved the great Steve wrong and that gave me tremendous satisfaction.

So Mum and I left for home, Mum promising to pop back later to see how Mrs Stone was getting on. That wasn't to be, however, because when we set off, Hairy came too.

"You see, he *does* want to be with you," Mum insisted.

"So why wouldn't he eat the food I offered him, then?"

"Why don't you take his bowl back to *your* house?" asked Mrs Stone. Mum thought this was positively inspired, but I thought the two of them were attaching far too much importance to the connection between Hairy and me. In the end, Mrs Stone crushed the tablets into the food and I dutifully carried it back to our place, plonked it in front of Hairy and went upstairs to work on the role of Mrs Johnson. When I came down about an hour later the food was still there, Hairy was still there, looking miserable, but Mrs Stone had gone.

"Where's Mrs Stone?" I asked.

"She's gone back to her place, because Hairy's going to stay here for a little while. I want to see if he'll start eating again."

"But look," I said, indicating the untouched food in the bowl. "He's *not* eating, is he? That proves it."

"You seem determined to prove the vet wrong, Lucy. Why is that?" Mum asked me, while giving me one of her level stares.

"I'm not trying to prove anything," I replied quickly.

Hairy had come over to me again and was licking my hand. "Stupid old thing," I said lightly, stroking his head, which he tried to get under my hand again the moment I stopped stroking him.

Mum sighed and went out. I sat on the floor and absent-mindedly started stroking the silly old thing again, while he wagged his tail and tried to sit on top of me. I went to the cupboard and got a bag of crisps out, then sat back down on the floor again cross-legged, with my faithful follower snuggled up to me, his head resting heavily on one of my legs. I stayed like this for quite a few minutes, thinking out loud. After all, Hairy wouldn't have any opinion on what I ought to do to get out of the mess I'd got myself into, but, on the other hand, I didn't feel quite so silly talking out loud, because I wasn't exactly talking to myself. I was talking to Hairy.

I told him all about what a pain the local vet

was, and how I hoped I'd never have to set eyes on him again, then I told him that on the other hand I desperately wanted to have my five friends back but I didn't know how on earth to go about it.

"What would you do? Hmm?" I asked him and he chose that moment to do a big stretch and open his mouth wide.

"I know I'm boring, but you might at least *pretend* to be interested," I told him, then I suddenly noticed how thin he was. "Look at you, you're a bag of bones," I said, ruffling his hairy coat. "I'll have to call you scrag bag," I went on. I smiled at the ridiculousness of the situation. "Look, Hairy, from one scrag bag to another, you've just got to eat something, you know. You're worse than me, you are. Come on." And I brought the food bowl over to him and sat in front of him, munching crisps.

At that moment the back door opened and in walked Terry. I jumped up to greet him and Mum came in to join us, but she didn't say a word to Terry because she was too busy staring open-mouthed at Hairy.

It really was amazing! The stupid old dog was wolfing his food as though he was in an eating competition. As soon as he'd finished, Mum said, "Give him some biscuits, Luce. They're in the cupboard."

So I jumped up, got the dog biscuits out,

tipped several into the bowl, then stood back to watch him wolf all those down as well. When he'd finished he looked round at us all one by one. I was the last one and he barked at me and wagged his tail.

"The vet was right, you know, Luce. He said that Hairy needed to be quite confident that you were going to stay with him before he'd eat. And that's the longest you've ever stayed still with him in the same room, isn't it?" Mum insisted.

Reluctantly, I was beginning to agree with her, but I was determined never to admit it to anyone, especially not to Steve.

Hairy stayed at my side for the rest of the evening and even wanted to come up to bed with me, but Mum said he had to get used to sleeping in his basket in the kitchen.

"Get used to it? Are we keeping him, then? I thought you didn't want him around?" I challenged her. "And what about your catering? It's not very healthy having a big slobbering dog around the place, is it?"

"He doesn't slobber," Terry defended Hairy.

"I didn't think *you* were all that keen, either," I said to Terry.

"I'd rather have a dog than a pair of rats, that's all," he said, then a look flashed between Mum and Terry.

"What's that look supposed to mean?" I asked.

"Well, the thing is," Mum began carefully, "Terry and I have been talking, and it's obvious we couldn't be so cruel as to get rid of Hairy, when he so obviously wants to stay here. But that leaves Mrs Stone with nobody, and she's made it perfectly clear she loves the rats, so we wondered whether or not you'd agree to a sort of ... well ... swap?"

Mum's shoulders were all hunched. She was obviously really worried about how I would react to this suggestion. I didn't mind at all if Mrs Stone had the rats. I'd never really wanted them in the first place and they only made me think of Steve every time I looked in their cage.

"Mrs Stone can have the rats, sure," I replied.

"Oh, great!" said Terry. "Well, that was easy," he added, with a wink for me and a smile for Mum.

"And what about Hairy?" Mum asked.

"I don't really care," I said. And it was true. I didn't. I had much bigger things on my mind, and if it made everybody else happy I didn't mind going along with it.

So the great exchange was made and Mrs Stone came round straight away to collect her new pets. You should have seen her. She was like a little girl, all excited and smiley. Her last words before she carried them off to her house were, "I'm going to train them, you know. I've been reading up about rats and you can get them to follow you round the house and round the garden!"

After she'd gone Mum and Terry burst out laughing, but I didn't. There was too much going on in my head. I went up to bed and lay there wide awake for ages and ages. I was trying to make a plan. Things were always better if you made a plan. But no plan would come into my head, and in the end I snapped on my light and saw that it was two o'clock in the morning. I didn't think I'd ever get to sleep, and in a way I didn't want to, because then I'd have to wake up and remember that I'd got no plan. And no plan meant no solution to my problems.

Everything seemed so bleak and empty that I started to cry. After a bit, I tried to pull myself together and decided to go downstairs and get a drink. I'd forgotten all about Hairy but I soon remembered as I went downstairs because through the kitchen door I could hear *him* crying.

In the hall I passed the mirror and caught a glimpse of my tear-stained face. *What a ridiculous situation!* I thought. *I'm miserable because I want my friends back, and Hairy's miserable because he probably thinks I've gone again and left him. Oh, poor Hairy!* I stood still and stared in the mirror. Then, like a thunderbolt, another terrible realization hit me hard and made me want to burst into tears all over again. How could I have shut myself off from this poor dog when he'd made it so obvious he was desperate to be with me? It was another of those things that I'd handled really badly over the past few days. I rushed into the kitchen, bent down and put my arms around his thin, trembly body.

"It's all right, Hairy, I'm still here. I'm not leaving you again, I promise."

He licked my face and the crying stopped. His tail wagged and he tried to sit on me again. All he succeeded in doing was knocking me off balance, so there we were, lying on the floor together, a thin dog and a thin girl. I couldn't help smiling at the whole thing, then gradually my smile turned into a laugh and I giggled until I ached with the strain of trying not to wake anybody up with my sudden bout of hysteria. Hairy obviously found my laughter infectious because he started barking and rushing round me in crazy excitement. I hugged him tight and told him to be quiet. There was still a big lump in my throat and I couldn't help a few more tears running down my face as I thought about all I'd put poor Hairy through.

"Don't worry, Hairy, I'll look after you properly from now on," I whispered as I hugged him tight, and he bobbed his head up and down, and shuffled around trying to get closer and closer to me, as if he couldn't get enough of my hugs and love. Then a few minutes later we crept upstairs together and Hairy clambered up on to my bed when I got in.

"Ni-night, Hairy. Sleep well."

He felt heavy on my feet so I bunched myself up more and he wriggled himself round and round until he was all cosy in the hollowed out bit he'd made. Then we must have both gone to sleep.

Chapter 10

The next morning, when I woke up to find Hairy, or Harry as I'd decided to call him, on the end of my bed, I immediately felt comforted. I reached out my hand to stroke him and he licked it lazily, then jumped rather floppily off the bed and stood by my door wagging his tail.

We went downstairs together and Mum gave me a brief lecture on how she didn't mind just that once, but in future Harry ought to sleep downstairs. I didn't argue but I'd no intention of letting him sleep downstairs until he knew he was here to stay and that I wasn't going to go off and leave him again. He ate a big bowl of food and a few biscuits, and I ate two pieces of toast and jam.

I begged Mum to let me stay off school just for that one day, because of Harry. She was on the point of refusing point blank when Terry came down and said to Harry, "What was all that crying about then? I heard you in the middle of the night. You're worried that your number one lady is going to go and leave you, aren't you, hmm?"

Then he turned to Mum. "I'm surprised he didn't wake you. It was the most awful ear-piercing whining. I was on the point of going downstairs myself, but, thank goodness, Luce heard him and went down."

I saw Mum looking more hesitant then, and I knew exactly what she was thinking. She was imagining how awful her long day at home, trying to cook with a whiney piney dog around, was going to be. Good old Terry. He couldn't have made a better speech at a better moment. I held my breath and waited for the verdict.

"Oh, all right. Just this once. And I really mean that, Lucy." She obviously did too because she only *ever* calls me Lucy when she's deadly serious. "After the whole day with you, surely he'll realize you're not planning on deserting him."

Good. I didn't have to worry about seeing the others for another day. I took Harry for a long walk in the morning and we went round to see Mrs Stone in the afternoon. She was overjoyed with the improvement in his appearance, and she was also very excited about what she'd achieved in such a short time with her rats. Harry and I watched the demonstration in amazement. Harry stayed glued to my side because I think he was afraid that he was coming back to live with Mrs Stone, but as it happened it was a good job he did so because it was obvious he was tempted to run after the rats. The rats were walking round the garden behind Mrs Stone, like ducklings after the mother duck. It had to be the funniest sight I'd ever seen. I laughed till the tears ran down my face, while Mrs Stone grinned her head off and kept asking me, didn't I think she was clever?

Later in the afternoon, I asked Mum in fear and trepidation whether I was allowed to go to drama. I was dreading her saying no because I shouldn't be seen at a drama class when I hadn't been to school, but she surprised me by saying, yes definitely, because I would be back at school the next day, after all. She also agreed to let me take Harry with me.

Sally looked pleased to see me, I thought, and I sat Harry in the corner where he stayed quite happily when I went off with the rest of the class. I felt very nervous because I wasn't sure if I was going to be allowed to try out as Mrs Johnson, but after a few minutes, Sally said, "Right, now the part of Mrs Johnson… Do you want a go at this or not, Lucy?" I could tell she thought I was going to say no, because she looked completely taken aback when I said yes.

"Would you like to try one of the songs first?"

I nodded and stood at the front. I focused on the clock at the back and thought about Mrs Johnson and her sad plight. The accompaniment on the cassette started and I began to sing. My eyes never left the clock, but it wasn't the clock I was seeing, it was the film of Charlie and the faces of Mrs Gadsby and of Bella. By the time I'd nearly finished the song, I was feeling so drained of emotion that I could hardly sing. I just held on, knowing it was almost over, and as the last notes faded away on the cassette my gaze slipped from the clock and I looked down.

The next thing I heard was loud, *loud*, clapping which made me jump because I wasn't expecting it. Then Sally was at my side, also clapping, and shaking her head slowly with tears in her eyes.

"I never knew you had it in you, Lucy. Well, that's not quite true. I *did* know you had it in you, but I thought you'd lost it, and now I see you haven't. So well done, you've got the part!"

The clapping subsided and I looked around me happily. Lots of the other girls and boys in the class congratulated me and patted me on the back, saying "Well done" as I walked over to Harry. Sally was carrying on with the try-out for another part so I decided to have a little moment with Harry, but before I got to him I was aware that someone was watching me from the door, which was open. I looked up and got the shock of my life because there, framed in the doorway, was Steve.

I couldn't pretend I'd not seen him, so I just stood there feeling stupid again.

"That was absolutely incredible, Lucy!" were his first words. I was so used to hearing him being critical that at first I thought he must mean incredibly bad. I bit my lip and looked down, and he came right up to me and put his hand on my shoulder.

"It *was* incredible, Lucy. You've got a real talent there, you know."

I looked up at him and saw that he was actually smiling. "Thank you," I said, then I stuck my hand out to Harry and he came over and put his two front paws on my legs, which meant that Steve had to move away a bit. I was glad, because it was too embarrassing having him being nice to me *and* close to me. Life's so strange, I thought. A week ago I would have given anything to have him that close and now I preferred Harry by a mile.

"What a transformation!" he said, after a moment.

I blushed, thinking he was talking about me, but then realized instantly that, of course, he meant Harry. "I can honestly say that I've never seen quite such an amazing recovery in a dog. He was in an awful state ... and now look at him.

That's because of you, Lucy. You've done that because of your affinity with him."

I looked up then and expected to see him laughing at me, taking the mickey out of my imaginary talent, but he wasn't even smiling. He looked totally serious. "You *have* got an affinity with animals, Lucy. At least, you have with this particular animal. It's a very special gift…"

Thank goodness I'd got Harry to stroke and make a fuss of, otherwise I would have been the colour of a beetroot. With every word he spoke, I was feeling happier and happier. I'd impressed him because of something *real*, something I'd really got, something I'd really done, not because of something I'd tried to be.

"You're rubbish with rats, though."

I stopped in the middle of stroking Harry and looked up again, abruptly. The look on his face made me want to crack up. He was on the point of laughing himself but we both knew we couldn't because at the front someone was auditioning, and it would have been awful to make any noise at all, so we had to stifle our giggles. I'll never forget that moment. It was magic. In the end, we crept outside so that we could talk without disturbing the class. Sally wouldn't mind. She was deep into her trials.

"I've been talking to Jan, Lucy," Steve said, after a moment.

The name made me go cold. I didn't want to talk about Jan. I wanted to stay in my lovely magic *Steve likes me after all* mood.

"And Jan's been talking to your mum…"

The blush, which had left my face, came creeping back. I felt as though Steve knew all about me now, and how weak and pathetic I was.

"You've been through a bad time, Lucy, and I just wanted to say that I'm sorry. I've been far too hard on you."

"I've been stupid," I said, in scarcely more than a whisper, as I thought, *Thank goodness he can't mind-read. Thank goodness he doesn't know how it all started. All because I fancied* him!

"All the best people are stupid sometimes, because they take risks and do outrageous things, and have ridiculous emotions. But that's what makes them so interesting, you see."

I thought about what he was saying for a moment, and that lovely feeling that it was all right after all – that I'd been stupid, but it was all part of being interesting – came flooding through me. And the best feeling of all was the realization that I liked Steve now. It wasn't because he was saying nice things about me, it was because I liked him for what he was.

"Can you bear to take one more risk?" he asked me.

"What is it?"

"Come to the café with me. Your friends are there."

"I've got drama."

"I know, but I want you to come to the café."

"I'm … not sure…"

"Go on…"

So I went back in and asked Sally if she'd mind if just this once I could go early. She said it was absolutely no problem because she would be auditioning till the end of the session and we'd start proper rehearsals the following week. So off we went, Steve and Harry and me. We talked about films and shows nearly all the way. I was amazed at how much Steve knew about acting and musicals and things, and he was so easy to talk to as well.

As we neared the café, I began to feel nervous.

"What shall we do about Harry?" I asked him. "Dogs aren't allowed in the café and I don't want Harry to think I'm leaving him again. He trusts me and I can't let him down."

"You've certainly come a long way," Steve said, with a smile. "Tell you what, I'll walk round with Harry for a little while. Ten minutes all right?"

"But I don't want to go in there on my own," I protested, feeling afraid all of a sudden.

"Go on. You'll be all right," he insisted; then we were there and he'd opened the door for me and walked off with Harry, so I had no choice.

Most of the tables in the café seemed to be empty, but at one big table sat Tash, Fen, Andy and Leah, which meant that Jaimini was working. Tash and Jaimini had obviously made some arrangement of their own. I felt totally conspicuous when I walked in. What on earth was I doing there? I shouldn't have let Steve persuade me. I'd no idea what to say to anyone and I couldn't see Jan anywhere. Immediately Tash stood up and Fen dashed off to the kitchen. It was as though they had been waiting for me but weren't sure if I would appear.

"Fen's just getting Jaimini," Tash hurriedly told me, while Leah and Andy looked at me as though I was a Martian or something. In no time at all Jaimini appeared and smiled at me, a sort of nervous smile, the kind you might expect from your French penfriend that you'd only just met. I think that was the moment that I realized that everyone else was as worried as I was. Jaimini and I sat down at one of the tables for two, and Jaimini started talking in a slow, stilted way that was nothing like the way she normally spoke.

"I thought you didn't like me any more."

"I've not been myself. I only know that now, you see…"

"I know … and I'm sorry, because I didn't realize and…"

"It's OK, it's my fault… I shouldn't have asked

you to help me with the rats, and anyway the whole rat thing was stupid…"

"No, it's my fault because I *did* know there was something wrong but I didn't realize you couldn't help it…"

"All the same, it's my fault because I should have… Well, I was going to apologize but then Steve started getting cross with me…"

"No…"

"No…"

There was a silence and neither of us knew what else to say.

"Friends?" asked Jaimini.

"Course," I said. "It's been the worst thing of all, not having you."

"Oh, Luce, I'm so sorry, I'd no idea… Let's make a pact."

"What sort of a pact?"

"A trust pact."

"Yeah, OK. It'll be my second trust pact in two days."

"Who was the first one with?"

"Harry, my dog."

"So he's *your* dog now?"

"Yeah, he's *my* dog, for ever."

Again, there was a silence. I didn't know what else to say. I felt suddenly very grown up, and I think Jaimini didn't know how to cope with this new me. I wanted to tell her that it was nothing permanent. I was just going through a serious phase in my life, but nothing had changed. I was the same old crazy Luce underneath it all, but I couldn't find the words to tell her. I looked round and saw that Jan was hovering nearby.

"Hello, pet, welcome back," she said. "The closed sign is on the door so I think we can break the rules and let your new-found friend in."

I glanced at the door and saw that Steve was standing there.

"You mean, you're actually going to let a *vet* in?" I said, with a giggle. This had the immediate effect of making everyone else burst out laughing, so that when Steve came in and everyone was laughing at him, he instantly wanted to know what the joke was.

"Jan said she was going to break the rules and let my new-found friend into the café," I told him, still giggling inanely.

"Room for one more?" said another voice from outside, and there was Donna.

"The more the merrier," Jan said.

Donna went up to Steve, stood on tiptoe, and gave him a kiss, and I saw to my horror that he was bringing her straight over to me. Oh well, I suppose she had to be faced at some point.

"It was totally my fault about the rats, Donna. I'm really sorry you felt so bad…"

"No, it was my fault," she cut in. "I shouldn't

have been so impetuous, rushing over there and grabbing your property without ever thinking that you might have got another rat. Steve and I had no idea that you were planning a surprise for us, and I went and spoilt the whole thing. I was lucky to get off so lightly with Jan. She's such a kind, fair person. I'd love to work for someone like that. My boss is a power lady who clicks her fingers and we all come running."

It's funny how you can get people so wrong, isn't it? I thought Donna would *be* a boss. I was convinced that *she* would be the power lady clicking her fingers and making everyone obey her. But there was something else she had said that was uppermost in my mind. *Steve and I had no idea that you were planning a surprise for us…*

But Steve knew *exactly* what I had been up to. That look he had given me when the second rat appeared. If looks could kill I would have been dead in that instant. And what was it he had said? *You deliberately led us to believe there was only one rat in there. I presume you were going to try and impress us by pretending the calm rat and the restless rat were one and the same…* Steve had despised me most of all at that moment, I think, but Donna hadn't realized how I'd planned to trick them, and Steve hadn't told her. He'd let Donna take the blame for something that was really *my* fault. Why? I just had to know.

There were lots of excited pockets of chatter all over the place, but Steve was on his own, stroking Harry. I went over to him and he straightened up and smiled. I spoke softly, but quickly, before I could change my mind.

"You knew why I'd got two rats instead of one. You knew it was *my* fault that the second rat escaped, because I didn't own up to it, but you never told Donna, did you? You let her take the blame? Why?"

He took a deep breath.

"Because you learn a lot about people when you're a vet. I suppose it comes from studying the links between pets and their owners, or maybe it's just me. I've always been interested in what makes people tick. There was something about you that intrigued me from the very first moment I set eyes on you, and when you spoke to me after that talk I did at your school, I knew you weren't telling me the truth. I could just tell. But, as I say, I was intrigued. I wanted to know why you needed to draw extra attention to yourself when you'd already got the looks that would instantly make people look twice…"

"You think people would look twice at me?"

"Yes, of course. Your face is full of character."

"*That* was my problem. I thought people looked at all my friends, but not at me, and then I thought if I got thinner…"

"Yes, I know. I talked to Jan, remember, and she's talked to your mum. But I'm not so stupid that I didn't work out that someone who goes to the lengths that you did to convince a vet that she's got an affinity with rats must have a lot going on inside her head, and I decided that you could probably do without getting into trouble with Jan, too, so I decided to let Donna take the blame. She's a grown woman. She can take it, and she did. Look."

I followed his gaze, and there were Jan and Donna laughing, with their heads close together.

"So Jan was never cross with me at all?"

"Not as far as I know. She's just been worried sick about you but wasn't sure whether it was her business to say anything."

So all those looks of Jan's which I had interpreted as cross looks were actually just seriously concerned looks. I really had been getting things wrong... It was as though my brain wasn't working properly. And I suppose that was about it. Your brain needs nourishment, like the rest of your body, and I had denied myself nourishment.

There was a tapping on the door, and, through the glass, I could see Mrs Gadsby trying to attract Jan's attention. She hadn't spotted me. Jan ran over and let her in.

"Is it a party?" asked Mrs Gadsby, smiling round.

"No, just a happy gathering," Jan said.

"Hello, Lucy. I thought I might find you here."

"She's a very sought-after girl, is Lucy," said Steve, putting an arm round me and giving me a squeeze. I saw Leah and Jaimini look at each other enviously at that moment. Then I caught Jaimini's eye, and she gave me her special smile and came over to me.

"I hope you don't get so popular that you forget your best friend," she said lightly. But I'd come a long way in a short time, and I had learnt to read the signs. However lightly she'd spoken I knew she wasn't feeling like that.

"I'll never forget my best friend. We made a pact, remember?"

Then I saw Tash and the others watching Jaimini and me from across the room. I went straight over to them, dragging Jaimini along by the hand.

"Sorry, Luce," said Andy simply, turning her big eyes on me. She never wastes words.

"Me, too," Fen added softly, and Leah just touched my arm.

"Me, too," I replied, then I turned to Tash. "Especially to you, Tash. You've been so kind all the time I've been having my brainstorm, and all I've given you back is nastiness."

"I only wanted you to be friends with Jaimini. You know what I'm like. I have to have a peaceful world."

"Well, we are friends. Best friends, in fact. See."

I was about to put my arm round Jaimini's shoulder to prove my point when Harry came galloping over, hurled himself at me and knocked me into Jaimini. We both fell over backwards and landed in a strange-looking heap on the floor.

"I think Harry must have heard you, Luce," said Steve, grinning. "He thought *he* was your best friend, you know."

"Yes, I've trained him to understand every word I say," I informed Steve jokingly from my glamorous position on the floor. "In fact, I'm going to re-christen him Brainy."

"So that's two brainy best friends you've got," commented Fen, with a giggle.

"Yeah, they're both brainy, but I think Harry's got the edge in the looks department," I answered her, with a wink. Then I gave Jaimini a big hug, which made Tash smile and made Jan say "Welcome back, Luce," for the second time that day. Only this time she added, "We've missed you."

Join

Would you and your friends like to know more
about Fen, Tash, Leah, Andy, Jaimini and Luce?

We have produced a special bookmark for you to
use in your Café Club books. To get yours free,
together with a special newsletter about Fen and
her friends, their creator, author Ann Bryant,
and advance information about what's coming
next in the series, write (enclosing a self-
addressed label, please) to:

The Café Club
c/o the Publicity Department
Scholastic Children's Books
Commonwealth House
1-19 New Oxford Street
London WC1A 1NU

We look forward to hearing from you!